PENGUIN BOOKS

the bay of contented men

Robert Drewe was born in Melbourne and grew up on the West Australian coast. His novels and short stories have been widely translated, won many national and international prizes, and been adapted for film, television, radio and the theatre. He has also written plays, screenplays, journalism and film criticism, and edited two international anthologies of stories. He lives with his family in Sydney.

ROBERT DREWE

the bay of contented men

PENGUIN BOOKS

Penguin Books Australia Ltd
487 Maroondah Highway, PO Box 257
Ringwood, Victoria 3134, Australia
Penguin Books Ltd
Harmondsworth, Middlesex, England
Penguin Putnam Inc.
375 Hudson Street, New York, New York 10014, USA
Penguin Books Canada Limited
10 Alcorn Avenue, Toronto, Ontario, Canada M4V 3B2
Penguin Books (NZ) Ltd
Cnr Rosedale and Airborne Roads, Albany, Auckland, New Zealand
Penguin Books (South Africa) (Pty) Ltd
5 Watkins Street, Denver Ext 4, 2094, South Africa
Penguin Books India (P) Ltd
11, Community Centre, Panchsheel Park, New Delhi 110 017, India

First published by Pan Macmillan Australia Pty Ltd 1989
This edition published by Penguin Books Australia Ltd 2001
Offset from the Picador edition

1 3 5 7 9 10 8 6 4 2

Cover design and digital imaging by Ellie Exarchos
Cover images by Getty Images and photolibrary.com
Printed and bound in Australia by McPherson's Printing Group, Maryborough, Victoria

National Library of Australia
Cataloguing-in-Publication data:

Drewe, Robert, 1943– .
The bay of contented men.

ISBN 0 14 100796 6.

I. Title.

A823.3

www.penguin.com.au

ACKNOWLEDGEMENTS

Thanks to Ray Lawrence for the archipelago, and Jane Camens for the bay.

Some of these stories were written while I held a fellowship from the Literature Board of the Australia Council, for which I want to record my appreciation.

Earlier versions of five stories, some with different titles, appeared as follows: 'Mandalay' in *Bondi*; 'The Lawyers of Africa' in the *Sydney Morning Herald* Literary Supplement and *Antipodes*; 'Life of a Barbarian' in *The Sydney Review*; 'The Hammett Spiel' in *Meanjin*; and 'The Bay of Contented Men' in *Xpress*.

R.D.

For

Veronica Brady
Jan Garvan
Jill Hickson

*A special harmony marked relations among the inhab-
itants. Wives and children were treated even more
gently here. These men loved their surroundings, their
neighbours and themselves. In a part of the world
where everyone seemed reasonably satisfied, these
reached the pinnacle of content. Maclay named the
group the Archipelago of Contented Men.*

E.M. Webster, *The Moon Man*, a biography
of the explorer, ethnographer and naturalist
Nikolai Miklouho-Maclay.

CONTENTS

RADIANT HEAT

MY mother heard it on the radio. They found the boy's body at 4.30 when they were packing up the picnic things, in a metre of water where the bottom of the lagoon shelved suddenly. In the panic it took them twenty minutes to think of counting heads. Then they discovered that another little boy was missing.

The second underwater search in thirty minutes. One child drowned, then another. It's too affecting a beginning, too much to accept. I feel uncomfortable ordering it so definitely. Wise after the event as usual. Full of selective certainties. But I know the second boy was a year younger than the first. Aged six. Lawrence Barker. I forget the first boy's name but obviously I remember Lawrence's. The compounded tragedy, the coincidences of the same name, age and place — Big Heron Lagoon — even their attending the same holiday child-care centre, saw to that. And my mother's reaction when she heard the news.

I'd told her that it was Peter's and Jenna's week with me. I know I'd said they were staying with Lucy and me down at the coast. They were not with Ellen, not spending their holidays at the child-care centre as usual, they were with me. (Somehow my mother's generation has trouble linking the ideas of 'father' and 'children'.) And 'Lawrence' hardly sounds like 'Peter'. But in the drama of a news bulletin enough connections could be made. I could see her making the leaps of imagination and despair. She knew we'd borrowed a friend's cottage at Bundeena, and Bundeena abuts the Royal National Park where the boys had died. So she had plenty to go on. For a long half-hour she was convinced that her grandson had drowned at a badly supervised children's picnic. When she finally reached me on the phone, I had to repeat to her, 'Mother, I can see Peter from here. He's watching "Inspector Gadget". I'll call him to the phone if you like.'

I never called her Mother but I was terse with her. She didn't believe me. She was babbling. Actually, my hand was trembling on the phone. I felt stunned. Peter was sitting crosslegged on the floor in his pyjamas watching television, and yet this evening there was a drowned boy named Barker, aged six.

Another layer of coincidence was making my hands shake. Only the day before, Lucy and I had taken the kids into the park for a picnic by the same lagoon. While my mother sighed and tutted I was replaying the day in my mind like a film, and recalling every frame. I remembered exactly the way the bottom of the shallow lagoon fell away suddenly in the middle. The water was a quieter, creamier green where the fresh creek met the salty white sand of the ocean beach — where, in winter, the higher tides burst through into the lagoon. I could feel the sandy bottom falling away right then, shifting and oozing around my ankles, the cooler currents around my shins, and I kicked away from the water-filled silence. And while my mother gradually calmed down and I turned the conversation around to Christmas plans, it struck me that my supervision of the children had been less than total. Certainly I watched them while they played in the water, but I read a magazine at the same time. I felt warm and lazy. The sun was bright and heavy on my eyelids; I couldn't swear that I didn't close them once or twice. And when I eventually dived in, the water was so bracing after the thick air that I stretched out and swam for several minutes, around a bend and temporarily out of sight.

Frankly, at the time I knew the risk. It occurred to me and I swam on. Worse, I anticipated *something*.

I looked at Peter and Jenna, absorbed by the cartoon, amusement flickering on their cheeks. I stared at them. Peter's hair was wet and spiky from his bath; a trickle ran down his neck behind his ear. Now and then he hummed the 'Inspector Gadget' theme. Despite his dead boy's particulars he moved, he spoke. I went over and stroked his head. To keep things fair, I reached over and patted Jenna's, too. They didn't notice. A little later I began feeling guilty. Waves of guilt swept over me. But I couldn't dwell on the other parents, on what those families were doing right then. I could imagine, but I tried to put them out of my mind. And I succeeded. I was ruthless. I erased their anguish. I burned it out of the air.

Both my children are good swimmers now. That summer we had them coached, and they still train regularly. Swimming is Peter's only sporting interest. When adults ask his hobbies, he's apt to say, 'My hobby is imagination'. He's one of those sort of ten-year-olds. A sci-fi reader. A dreamy monster-lover. He moons through school classes but knows twenty ancient instruments of torture. He's a 'Dungeons and Dragons' buff. He likes those adventure books where the reader is the hero, and gets to decide which plot strand to follow. Already Peter wants to channel his fate, if only to choose the sword-fight with the skeleton ahead of the possible mauling by the werewolf.

LUCY and I moved to the coast ourselves last year, north rather than south, escaping from city real estate prices as much as other tensions. We bought a cottage at Springstone, a renovated weekender whose high position on Blackwall Hill we believed would compensate for its drawbacks. The views of the bay even made up for the mosquitoes and sandflies which rose from the reeds and mangrove flats at low tide and settled on the house. 'Citronella Heights,' I joked. Lucy is a member of the post-pesticide generation, an advocate of citronella oil as an insect repellent. Last summer we'd spray ourselves before drinks in the garden, before going to the beach, even — especially — before bed. The pungent citronella oil soaked into our clothes, sheets, furnishings, car upholstery. I didn't mind it; the fragrance was nostalgic. It brought back serene times, patchouli oil and incense and women in caftans. But everyone entering our house or car would ask, 'What *is* that smell?'

The children had no faith in citronella. They liked the way pesticides *annihilated* mosquitoes. One Saturday Peter woke with a badly bitten forehead and puffy eyelids. He was struck with awe and admiration for the face in the mirror ('I look like a halfling, a demi-human.

I told you that stuff didn't work.'). But his ogre's demeanour had lapsed by bedtime. The first mosquito whine made him frantic. 'They're coming for me!' he yelled. We allowed him dispensation: he was permitted the old poison.

Destruction can be enjoyable, especially with right on your side. It's hard to put more than the broadest Buddhist case for the mosquito. A day I remember from last spring, the Monday of a holiday long-weekend: the arrow on the gauge outside town pointed to Extreme Fire Danger; in the way of city people I was heeding the warning and clearing the bush around the house. What I was doing was really more drastic than clearing. I was hacking into the lantana and scrub with the new Japanese brush-cutter. I was razing things flush to the earth. My blade screamed. Insects flew from the din and lizards scuttled in panic. In the trees above me, lines of kooka-burras conspired patiently to swoop on newly exposed centipedes. I was righteous in my destruction: the lantana is an introduced pest, the centipede's bite is painful and poisonous, and so on. I stomped through the scrub wielding the cutter. Rock shards bounced off my heavy-plastic protective glasses, branches snapped underfoot. 'You look like "The Terminator",' Peter said. He approved. He was swinging a scythe. It was too big for him but he swung it anyway. The Grim Reaper, of course, and pleased to be him.

This was the month of unseasonal heat when people in shops and at bus stops first began talking about the Greenhouse Effect. Arsonists were lighting fires in the national parks, and an infestation of Bogong moths, blown by the north-westerlies, descended on the city and coast. The moths had become disoriented on their migration south from Queensland to the alpine country. They turned up in every building. They crawled into cupboards and kettles and shoes, into the luggage lockers in aircraft cabins and the more sinuous wind instruments of orchestras. They flew hundreds of miles out to sea before dropping in the waves. Some made it to New Zealand. Cats and dogs got fat and bored with eating them. (They were big and calorific; on windscreens they splattered into yellow grease.) Everyone had moths, and those places where bottlebrush trees were flowering for spring — the moths' favorite food was bottlebrush nectar — had a hundred times more.

In the hot wind the moths rose in a flurry from our bottlebrushes and showered red pollen on my son's head. Lucy and Jenna had left us to our mayhem. We cut and slashed and raked, but eventually stopped to have a drink. Peter was still charged with an edgy friskiness. While I drank a beer he entertained me with his repertoire of murderous noises and death scenes. He mimed axes in skulls and arrows in throats. He did blow-pipes and bazookas. He lurched about with his red-tinged hair, grunting and gurgling. He switched roles from killer to victim. Bullets ricocheted off rocks, scimitars flashed. He could crumple to the ground a dozen ways, holding his entrails in.

The air on our hill was yellow and smoky. Against the blurry horizon he filled me in on monsters. His favorites were the Undead — zombies, ghouls, wights, wraiths, mummies and skeletons. 'They're *chaotic*,' he said. What he liked about them, and gave him the creeps, was their potential for anarchy. Their evil was disorderly. Despite his patient explanations he lost me after that. The bushfires were on my mind and 'Dungeons and Dragons' is a complex game. But I've flipped through his guidebook, wondering at the attraction. 'A wraith looks like a shadow which flies, and *drains levels* as a wight. A mummy does not drain levels.' I'm none the wiser. I notice they all seem impervious to heroics. 'Ghouls are immune to *sleep and charm spells*. They are hideous beast-like humans who will attack any living thing. Any hit from a ghoul will paralyze any creature of ogre-size or smaller (except elves)...'

I knew zombies from those comedy-duo films of the fifties where they chased Abbott and Costello and Martin and Lewis. I knew Malcolm Rydge. This is an easy joke now that I can safely glance out of restaurant windows and not catch him looking in. I can walk the streets and not see him jog past, averting his eyes. I can leave my house suddenly without his car accelerating away. I can return the children to my old house, to Ellen, and not hear his excitable gabble in the kitchen, my name ringing in the air, the abrupt hush, the scramble for the back door.

There was finally a moment, a Friday lunch, when I looked down from the New Hellas, randomly, between mouthfuls of souvlakia, into Elizabeth Street. Malcolm was standing across the road in Hyde Park staring up at my window seat, my regular table. Our eyes met and held this time, in some sort of recognition. There is always someone who thinks you know the secret. Any secret. The secret of knowing Ellen first. The secret of the window table. Ellen had just thrown him out, he told me on my way out. He was waiting for me. It occurred to me later that he could have had a gun, a

21

knife, in that shoulder bag he always wore. He slipped up in his running shoes and shook my hand as if he liked me. His eyes were distracted. His skin was damp and flickery. She had someone else. The voodoo was over, at least for me.

Lucy doesn't scoff at unquiet spirits. Ellen shuts them all out. She drops the portcullis. Her father went for a walk after lunch when she was twelve and never came back. From the veranda she saw him disappear into the treeline, swinging his stick and eating a Granny Smith apple. No-one ever found anything. Before it was called Alzheimer's Disease, my mother's mother was always trudging into town to hand in her own belongings to the police. 'I found this handbag in Myer's,' she would say. 'Some lass *will* be in a state.' She basked in her honesty as the cops drove her home again. My mother used to examine her own behaviour for early signs. Now that she doesn't any longer, I do.

Is it a sign that she gets younger every year? That since her sixtieth birthday she's been in reverse gear, hurrying backwards from the end? In the nine years since, she's shed twelve — lopping them off like old branches. Soon she'll pass me coming the other way. And this fifty-seven-year-old Elizabeth (who must have given birth to me at fourteen!) has lately turned into Bettina, having arrived there via Betty and Beth. Doesn't she remember the big party, the guests, the witnesses to her turning sixty? That I gave a speech? That we made a fuss of her? 'What's up with Bet?' her old friends wonder. What can I say? Her old friends look seventy. 'Bettina' looks, well, a cagey fifty-eight. She began getting younger in the 1970s with everyone else. In the 1980s, when everyone else started ageing again, she wilfully stayed behind. Is this a sign? The chin lift? The capped teeth? The bag removals? Lots of purple and gold? Sudden yellow hair? Leopard-skin materials? 'Ocelot,' she says firmly. 'Not leopard, ocelot.' What's the difference? It's not as if it's real skin, animal fur. It's only fabric, cotton blend stretch or something. 'It's what leopard skin *stands for*,' my North Shore sister grumbles. 'She's no chicken.'

Why does Penny always bring our father into it, even into the question of the ocelot-print stretch pants, even nine years later? Because our mother began getting younger as soon as he died? Well, she looked old for a month or two, for appearances' sake, then she started going backwards. 'I just know what Dad would say,' Penny says. But she never says what he'd say ('I'd prefer not to see those pants on you, Betty.') 'Maybe he'll let us know,' I could say to Penny. In one of his posthumous letters with the yellow stamps shaped like bananas and a Tonga postmark.

THAT afternoon the wind carried the sound of fire sirens from the expressway to the coast. They closed the expressway to traffic when the fire jumped the six lanes and surged eastward. From our hill the western sky was a thick bruised cloud fading to yellow. The eucalypts around the house suddenly began to peel. The hot winds had dried and cracked their bark and given the trees a strange mottled look, as if they'd pulled on camouflage uniforms. Now the bloodwoods and peppermints and angophoras were peeling and shedding fast in the wind, dropping sheets of bark all around us, changing their colour and shape before our

23

eyes. Some trees revealed themselves as orange, others were pink, yellow, even purple underneath. All of them seemed moist and vulnerable, membrane instead of wood. They looked as if they'd shiver if you touched them.

All the bushfire-warning literature talks about 'radiant heat'. I'd read that radiant heat was the killer factor in bushfires and I wondered if the trees peeling was some sensitive early-warning system, an early stage of radiant heat. People can't survive more than a few kilowatts of radiant heat touching them. I read that to stand in front of a fire only sixty metres wide was like being exposed to the entire electrical output of the State of Victoria at peak load. Every single metre of this sixty metres beams out the heat of thirty-three thousand household radiators! And now it seemed to be getting hotter even as the sun got lower.

Wary of Peter's vivid imagination, I kept quiet about radiant heat. With the growing clouds of smoke, the trees changing, his eyes were already skittish. 'What holiday is it supposed to be today?' he asked me. Labor Day? I couldn't remember. On rare days things come together: heat, a moth plague, fires, crowds of people. When random factors combine you anticipate more things happening. The drowning tragedy on the news. Maybe the arrival of a letter, mailed from some dozy South Pacific port six months before, from a father five months dead. ('I think the cruise has done me the world of good.') Peter made poison darts fizz through the air, *phht, phht, phht.* 'Let's get out of here,' he said.

In Australia people always run to the coast. Maybe the myth of the bush is a myth. In the car we had less than a kilometre to travel. The heat and the closed

windows had activated the citronella oil in the upholstery. It felt like breathing citronella into one lung and
smoke into the other.

At the beach we found Lucy and Jenna in the crowd
by the rock pool. Everyone seemed to have the same
idea. People brushed away moths as they laughed
nervously about the smoky wind. Dead moths littered
the high-tide line, moths and bluebottles that had been
washed ashore. The bluebottles' floats, electric-blue
and still full of air, were sharp and erect as puppies'
penises. There was a rotting smell from a pile of dead
shags. The force of the westerly had flattened the surf;
the waves were low and snapping and plumes of
spindrift shot away from the beach. People had put up
windbreaks, and lounged behind them, facing the sea
and drinking beer. One group was drinking champagne and giggling.

'What's that red stuff in Peter's hair?' Jenna said.

'Pollen,' I said. 'From the moths.'

'It'll wash off in the sea,' Lucy said.

AT sunset the wind dropped suddenly and by the time
we needed to leave for the city the expressway was
open again. It was early evening. Jenna and Peter had
to return to school the next day, back to Ellen's. I was
sorry the expressway had reopened. It would have
been an excuse to keep them for a while. Maybe they'd
have been stuck with me for days, with the road closed,
the lines down. We would have been safe enough. We
could always run into the sea.

Lucy kissed us goodbye. The narrow road out of
Springstone was clogged with cars, everyone leaving

at the same time. On the approach to the expressway the service stations all had fire trucks pulled into the back. Dirty fire-fighters slumped around the trucks, drinking from cans. One man was sitting on the ground trickling water from a hose over his head.

I pulled into the Shell station and filled the tank. I went inside and paid, and bought the kids some drinks. When I came out I noticed how badly the smoky wind and squashed moths had smeared the windscreen. I began to clean it. Just then a small Nissan truck came in fast and braked hard next to our car. A man in his late twenties jumped out of the driver's seat a few metres from me and headed around to the passenger side where a woman was screaming.

The woman was holding a boy of three or four on her lap. She was screaming in his face, 'You're going to die! Do you hear me? Die! Die!'

For a moment the man stood indecisively at the woman's window. He had wavy blond hair and he ran his hands through it and muttered something to the woman, something mild and self-conscious in tone, but she continued to scream at the child that he was going to die. The child looked stunned, as if he had just woken. I was standing there transfixed, with the squeegee in one hand and a wiper blade in the other. The man saw me looking and gave a wink. He took a couple of steps in my direction. 'Sorry, mate,' he said.

I didn't say anything. Through the windscreen I saw Peter's and Jenna's faces staring at the truck cabin. They both had shocked, embarrassed smiles. The man turned to go into the service station office, but the woman began screaming louder and hurling obscenities and he turned back to the truck.

It was no place to be. I was hurrying to finish the windscreen, but — isn't it always the way? — those splattered moths were stuck fast. I seemed to be working in slow motion. Although I was making brisk, fussy dabs at the glass nothing much was improving. I had a sudden inkling the woman was doing something cruel to the boy that the man and I couldn't see. She was dark-haired, dark-eyed, the man's age or a bit older, and the wide spaces between her front teeth showed when she screamed. The boy had her looks and colouring. It's odd hearing a woman calling a man a cunt, over and over. Peter and Jenna weren't smiling any more. Jenna was pale and cupped her hands over her ears. She was near tears, whereas Peter's expression was confused and distant. He looked straight ahead, blinked, tried a silly scowl. His face was off-centre.

'Die, die die!' the woman screamed again, and began to smack the little boy's face. He started to scream, too. The reaction of the blond man to her onslaught was so mild and understated as he leaned in the cabin window that two thoughts struck me: *that's not his child* and *what did he do or say to her just before this?*

'Please don't do that, you're hurting him,' he said as she continued to hit the boy's face. 'You're making him cry.'

I wanted the man to do something. I wanted him to stop shuffling on the driveway and take over. Do whatever's necessary, I willed him. Get tough with her. By now other motorists were pulling in and staring across at the disruption as they filled their tanks. Two teenagers sauntered past, snickering. I could see the lone service station employee peering out from behind the cash register. There was just enough room in the truck cabin for the woman to swing at the boy while she was holding him on her lap, and she began to punch his head.

'Hey!' I yelled. As if he'd been waiting for a complaint from the general public, the man leaned through the window and tried to grab her arm. She hit him with a flurry of punches, and her screeches and abuse rose in pitch. The boy screamed higher. The man stepped back from the truck and ran his fingers through his hair. 'I'm going for those cigarettes,' he announced, and walked inside the service station.

The woman stopped yelling and began rocking the boy on her lap. She stroked his cheeks, murmuring to him, and pulled his head down on her chest. Gradually, he stopped crying. I put the bucket and squeegee back beside the pumps. As I got back in the car she looked up and shot me a defiant glance. She was still glaring at me, muttering something, as we drove off.

Neither the children nor I said anything. My stomach felt queasy. While I was trying to think of something to say my stomach was turning over. Suddenly I couldn't bear the sickly smell of citronella in the car, the way the air-conditioner re-circulated and revived it. I opened my window to get some air. 'Open your windows,' I said. The smell of fire immediately came into the car. Little specks of ash floated in. Trees were smouldering on both sides of the expressway. Even the grass on the median strip was charred and off to the left flames glowed in a gully.

'Look down there!' I said. I was enthusiastic. I welcomed the diversion of the fire. 'It burned right through here, jumped the highway, and there it is now!'

'Wow,' said Peter, in a low voice. In the heavy traffic we were driving in the inside slow lane, well under the limit, peering out at the fire. The firemen had driven it up against a treeless sandstone ridge. It was fading fast without the wind behind it. But then light burst beside us and there was a roar. For an instant I thought *fire!* but it was the Nissan truck accelerating past us on the inside, on the narrow asphalt shoulder, showering us with loose stones. I saw the three profiles as they passed: the man driving with a cigarette in his mouth, the woman with the boy on her knees. The truck swung back on to the road, swerved around three or four other cars, shot into the outside lane and out of sight.

AFTER I took the children home I drove to my mother's flat. Sometimes I stay overnight with her and head back to the coast first thing in the morning. She has a spare bedroom I've been using for emergencies ever since she moved into the flat after Dad died. I was there for a month when Ellen and I broke up. It was after eleven when I got there this time. I was so drained I could hardly think.

She was in her red tracksuit and gold slippers eating toast. She had face cream on her forehead and cheeks. 'Oh, dear,' she said when she saw me. She extracted a tissue from her tracksuit pocket and wiped her face. 'How are you, dear?'

I quickly said I was fine. Often these days she asks

me questions and doesn't listen to the answers. I've just begun to answer and she's on to another question. Sometimes I have to say, 'Do you want to hear this or not? It's all the same to me. I'm just answering you.'

'I'm fine, Mum,' I said. 'I just need a brandy and I'll be fine.' I poured us both a drink and carried them into the living room. It's a small room; I sat next to her on the sofa. 'I was thinking of you watching the news,' I said. 'I hoped you wouldn't worry. The fires didn't get near us. Anyway, Peter and I cleared away all the scrub. No need to worry about fires reaching us.'

'What fires?' she said. 'I've been out. I went to see that Meryl Streep film. I thought she looked a bit horsey.'

'You always say she looks horsey!' I said. 'She's gorgeous. What do you mean, anyway, horsey?'

'You know, angular. Aquiline features or whatever they are. Equine.'

'Meryl Streep's beautiful! Can't you see that? She's the best film actress in the world.'

'Well, she's not my cup of tea,' my mother said. 'She was playing a booze artist, some Skid Row type.' She sipped her drink daintily. She still drinks alcohol in company like a guilty teenager, as if she's new to it, but there are always a couple of empty Remy Martin bottles when I take her garbage out.

'She was *acting*, Mum.'

'What's this about fires?' she said.

'It doesn't matter.' I took a big sip of brandy and swallowed it. 'The whole central coast nearly went up in flames. But it's under control now.'

'Oh, dear,' she said.

'It was weird. All our trees were cracking and peeling. Hot ash was flying everywhere. We escaped to the beach.'

'You must be careful, living up there.' She got up frowning and padded into the kitchen to make me more toast. 'It's the smoke you die from, not the flames,' she said.

'It's the radiant heat,' I said.

I could hear her out in the kitchen muttering something about smoke. 'Don't worry,' I called out. She was making familiar kitchen noises. I listened for her tutting sound, the anxious clicks her tongue made on her teeth when she did things for us. Things would come back to her: events, feelings, memories as organised as snapshots. When she brought me the toast she would lightly touch me on my head or shoulder. A little pat or squeeze. I was a war baby. He was away fighting in the Solomons. For two years it was just me and her. I sank back into the sofa and called out again, 'You really don't need to worry!'

MACHETE

AT eight this morning there was a machete lying on the lawn, flat in the middle of my front yard. It gave me a jolt. It's hard to describe the feeling of seeing a machete lying on your lawn when you're picking up the morning paper. I don't own a machete. It's not a common garden tool around here. In my mind a machete is a weapon of foreign guerillas. Rural terrorists. I associate machetes with the random slaughter of innocent villagers, the massacre of peasant farmers who backed the wrong party.

Well, I picked it up — my heart beating faster — and hefted it in my hand. The blade was heavy and sharp; it was in good order. All the while I couldn't believe it was there in my yard, in my hand. I was peering around to see if the machete's owner was about to appear but there were only the usual sleepy-looking suburban houses coming to life. People were backing cars out of their driveways and leaving for work; children were setting off for school; a woman down the street watered her garden. In a moment I began to feel self-conscious standing there in my suit and tie, all set for work, with the rolled newspaper in one hand and a machete in the other.

Belleview is a new suburb: Gillian and I moved here

six months ago but we don't know anyone yet. These sandy, gravelly plains on the outskirts of the city were never thickly vegetated, and the developers bulldozed those trees and bushes, mainly spindly acacias, which had persevered. The residents are just starting to establish their lawns and gardens, but it's a battle in the sand. Everything blows away, and when it rains your topsoil washes half a kilometre down the road. What I'm saying is that it's not tropical rainforest or anything. A rake, a spade and a pair of secateurs will see you through. There is no need for slashing and hacking.

So I was standing in the front yard holding the machete and thinking all sorts of imaginative things. How the machete came to get there in the middle of the night, and so forth. It's a long drive to work, to the bank, and I knew the highway would be jammed already, but now I'd found the machete I couldn't just leave.

My mind was whirling. Gillian left work three weeks ago, in her seventh month of pregnancy, and she would be at home, alone, all day. It was our first baby and she was in a state just being pregnant without me mentioning the machete.

So whose machete was it? I didn't know the neighbours, only that the other young couple on the right worked long hours and that the fellow on the left kept Rottweilers. His wife was Filipino and stayed indoors all the time. Her face peeping through the curtains looked wistful. We'd heard him shouting at night. My guess was that a Rottweiler owner was more likely to own a machete, and to care for it so well.

From where I was standing with the machete I lined

up the front door of the Rottweiler residence. There was only the low paling fence separating us. Someone could have thrown the machete from the front door to where I stood if they wanted, if they were impelled to do that. But it was hard to think of a reason why.

I couldn't see myself going next door past all the Rottweilers and asking, 'Excuse me, did you leave your machete in my yard? When you were trespassing last night?' By then it was well after eight and my one clear thought was not to frighten Gillian with any quirkiness. Things were making her weepy and anxious lately: all those children on TV with rare diseases, the hole in the ozone layer, fluoride in the water. I wanted to keep her serene. I took the machete around to the back of the house. I pushed it hard into the sandy flowerbed by the corner of the garage until only the handle stuck up, and that was hidden by shadow. Then I got into the car, drove to work and forgot about it.

But tonight as I was driving home past the Hardware Barn I remembered it. The strange feeling came back and I speeded up. These nights the sun sets well before five and our end of the street was in darkness when I pulled up. The Rottweiler house was dark, and our house too. I left the headlights on and ran to the back of the garage.

There is something more alarming than the presence of a machete. The absence of a machete.

THE FIRST MOTEL

THE manager of the first motel in the world isn't too worried about his cats getting flattened on the highway.

Halfway through negotiations, it's Clara, the stylist, who becomes distracted by the cats. She is Australian. Her attention keeps shifting to the runny-eyed kittens limping across the driveway or rolling, dazed, in the dusty oleanders. The traffic is roaring past a few feet away.

'It's so busy.' Clara says. 'Don't you lose some of your cats out there?'

The manager yawns. 'Sure we lose a lot, but we got plenty more.' He is sleepy, fat, black, in his mid-forties. His soft slurry voice barely carries over the noise of the trucks careering through Sun Valley. 'Eight hundred,' he says, avoiding Clara's eyes, her pale efficiency, by gazing over her towards the steam plant across the highway. 'Tell your producer eight hundred dollars a day.'

'It was six hundred yesterday,' Clara says.

The manager shrugs. 'The owner says eight hundred is rock bottom. We can get a thousand easy.' A smeary mirage quivering on the roof of the steam plant seems to have taken his attention. 'Hollywood

41

pays a thousand,' he says eventually. 'People from the east are happy to pay twelve hundred to use The First Motel. We had the French here one time, some Germans, the Japanese, they paid twelve hundred.'

Clara looks across to Martin, the producer, who is hovering in the vicinity of the negotiations. Martin likes to be adjacent to financial wrangling, aware of it but just a little aloof. First he makes a sound in his nose and then he nods to Clara. 'OK,' he says. 'O-*kay*.' His palms are raised in surrender. 'As the gentleman can see,' he says loudly, 'we're all geared up ready to shoot.' He waves an expansive arm. 'We've come thousands of miles from England to his motel on the under*standing* that the charge was six hundred a day.' He strides over to Clara and the manager, shaking his head and smiling tightly, but he doesn't look entirely dissatisfied. While his eyes don't meet theirs, they glitter as if some expectation has been met. He peels some notes from a wallet and hands them to the manager. 'Shall we get on with it?' he says, with the same smile.

Today they will shoot a commercial for British Airways. The motel will be seen in Britain as an icon of America. Nearly everyone is thrilled with the look of the place. A fortnight ago Clara, Patrick, the location manager, and Clive, the visual advisor, had almost given up their search for the perfect motel. They were heading back to the coast and the run-of-the-mill examples of the genre in Santa Monica and North Hollywood, when suddenly she saw it gleaming in the late afternoon sun. Pink.

'Pull over,' Clara said. 'That's it.'

She couldn't believe her luck. On the roof, in crimson neon, a sign said *The First Motel*. Underneath, in blue, it said *Vacancy*. They parked the hire car and prowled about, Clara making little gasps of surprise and delight at each discovery. She gasped at the six ornamental flamingos stuck into the patch of lawn by the office. She gasped at the fish-shaped swimming pool (empty). She gasped at the cafe with its soda fountain and vintage Coke signs.

'You're right,' Clive said.

'Not just a bit *too* tacky?' Patrick wondered. He was from the Golden Gate Bridge, Statue of Liberty, Grand Canyon generation of location managers.

'No, it's perfect,' she said. 'Look here.'

In the cafe window was a faded sign. It said, 'Welcome to the first motel in California, the United States and the World! Originally named the Sun Valley Motor Hotel, it was built in 1946 by Gene W. Underwood on his return from active duty. While serving in the Pacific, Gene Underwood had a vision. After the war he would build a roadside hotel for motorists — and where better than California, where the automobile thrived! Mr Underwood imagined that Hollywood folk would appreciate a weekend holiday in the scenic Valley, within easy driving distance. And he guessed right! The idea of the motor-hotel quickly caught on. Asked why he chose Sun Valley for the first 'motel', Gene Underwood always said, 'After two years in the Navy, I thought inland was the way to go!'

Clara couldn't wait for the first production meeting so she could tell Martin.

TODAY's shoot features two attractive British tourists, played by Stuart and Jane, who, according to the

43

script, will spot the motel sign, animate their faces and pull off the road to sample 'the real America'. They are driving a 1958 tundra-grey Oldsmobile convertible in showroom condition (two thousand dollars a day plus insurance). Timing is everything. Clive has recommended to Nick, the director, that they shoot the car scene just before sunset — when the light is interesting — and the motel establishing shot just after, when it is dark enough for the neon to be seen to advantage.

The eight hundred a day covers the use of a motel room for wardrobe and make-up and to shelter the actors from the elements. Shawna, the make-up artist, is gently dishevelling Jane when Clara enters the room with an armload of travelling clothes for the shoot and opens the wardrobe to hang them up. A whiff of ancient body odour hits her; some old jackets and trousers and polyester shirts are already hanging in there; something live rustles in a corner; Clara quickly shuts the door. Shawna is bright and nervy as usual, chewing gum as she back-combs Jane's hair. 'I bet these walls could tell some stories,' Shawna says.

'So could the carpet,' Jane says.

Clara lays the clothes on the bed. As she does so her hand grazes and recoils from the pumpkin-colored bedspread, some heavy synthetic fabric both coarsely-fibred and slippery and, she sees, spotted with dubious stains. Jane is full of witticisms but avoids her eyes. It seems no one is looking at Clara today. Last night Martin took Jane out to dinner, and now Stuart is sulking with Jane. This new American Stuart is slumped in front of the TV, aggressively swigging Coke and chewing beef jerky and watching baseball,

44

now and then shouting 'Heeey!' and 'You *ass*hole!' and 'Way to go!' at the players. In three weeks Stuart has left behind both irony and *arse*. Stuart went to Harrow; on-camera he's supposed to look like a middle-class Englishman. Off-camera he's got himself an American haircut and plaid, denim and down-filled outdoor clothes. He's dressed more for hiking in New England than for Southern California. He looks like someone out of Norman Rockwell or the L.L. Bean fall cata- logue. Nick is furious with him for getting a haircut halfway through a shoot. ('He only got the job because of his fucking cowlick! This is *totally* unprofessional. I'll put a fucking bowler hat on him if I have to.') And Martin hasn't spoken to her today except acidly about the eight hundred a day. It's as if Denver and San Diego and Sedona, Arizona hadn't happened — and the night before last in the Century Plaza.

So that she doesn't have to watch Jane being so easily glamorised, Clara wanders to the door and leans in the doorway. The safety chain has been ripped off the jamb. The haze outside is sweet with oil and rubber and brake linings, and shudders with traffic. A blonde woman in a bathrobe strolls past with an armful of sick kittens. Two thin toddlers sit very still under the oleanders. The manager's door is closed, with a *Do Not Disturb* sign on it. Across the driveway, a black man on crutches, an arm and a leg in plaster, gets out of his room with difficulty and drags himself to the cafe. In front of the cafe the crew is setting up the light and sound equipment; the sparks assistant is on the roof replacing the dim L in MOTEL with a brighter one. Without a sidelong glance, not even at the glistening

45

Oldsmobile, the man on crutches sidles past.

Inside the motel room, Jane declares, 'I intend to dance my tits off tonight.'

Clara departs briskly. Out on the driveway she looks for somewhere to go. It is imperative she be seen heading in a particular direction in a purposeful manner. The woman in the bathrobe passes her strolling the other way, the kittens still clasped to her chest. She looks through Clara and croons, 'Here, kitty, kitty. Yes, Momma's got her kitties.' Clara blinks in the pink reflected glare. Trucks, trailer-trucks, buses, hoot and rumble past into the vast illusive lake where the steam plant used to be. Where is Martin? Did she dream the Los Abrigados Hotel? Was the Century Plaza only thirty-six hours ago?

Martin's dark English form stands in front of the cafe. He is buttering up the two motorcycle patrolmen assigned to the shoot, laughing politely, probably gathering racy anecdotes for re-telling at home, for re-telling to Jane tonight. Nevertheless Clara finds herself suddenly standing with them staring at Martin's sublimely innocent face. The cops are gallant sergeants, removing their sunglasses and shaking her hand. One is fiftyish, tall and heavy, Irish-faced; the other is younger, shorter, edgier, with a weight-lifter's chest and biceps and a clipped macho moustache. They could be cops in a movie and look totally aware of it.

Martin must think so, too; Martin was *winking* at them. 'I guess a place like this is not exactly *unknown* to the police?' His accent sounded too eagerly English to Clara today. *Not exactly unknown.* What happened last night, winking street-wise Martin? *Look at me.*

The older sergeant is staring wistfully off across the

valley. 'Used to be a honeymoon hotel in the days before the area was Spanish,' he says.

'And now?' Martin keeps on. Gradually more blacks are entering the landscape. And Mexicans. A group of Mexicans is trudging along the edge of the highway and taking a short cut across the patch of grass in front of the motel. Men in work clothes, women with shopping bags, surly teenagers, some small children. They push solemnly through the oleanders. Oleander branches whip back and forth. The Mexicans are stepping over the lawn flamingos and the manager's sick cats and wearing a path in the dusty grass.

At the Los Abrigados Hotel she and Martin dined and danced to a mariachi band. When? This time last week? They were seven thousand feet above sea-level. Was she light-headed at that altitude?

'One big honeymoon now,' says the older sergeant, and laughs at something over their heads. As the sun sinks lower, black men are coming out of their motel rooms, yawning and stretching and gathering in the motel's turning circle. They have the optimistic air of the recently risen, of permanent residency and of a fresh day beginning. They ignore the film activity, the people hurrying and shouting and laying electric cord and setting up the camera. The preparation of the Oldsmobile, this finned beauty, arouses no interest. They bring out directors' chairs, light up cigarettes and open cans of beer.

'Victimless crime, it's a waste of everyone's time,' says the muscular cop, turning his helmet in his hands. He holds the helmet crooked lovingly in one arm, curls his biceps against it, then again, then surreptitiously switches arms. His eyebrows, Clara notices, are clipped to match his moustache. His edgy manner, his self-conscious stance, put her in mind of a nervous actor at a casting session. He was in awe of the business; he was *auditioning* as a tough cop.

The hum rises on the highway. The sky recedes to a rusty pink. Every so often a vehicle from the peak-hour traffic — a pickup truck, a big battered sedan — peels off the road and turns into the motel, weaving around the Oldsmobile and the crew, and lines up by the casual group of men in the courtyard. Money and packages change hands without anyone leaving their vehicles.

On the set there is the usual flurry. Nick is waving his arms at the grip and gaffer, both Americans. 'Do you understand what I'm saying?' he asks them loudly. 'Do you have the faintest inkling what I'm talking about?' Martin notices none of this. He seems rooted to the spot, as if he's using the police as a buffer between him and her. The older sergeant is saying that Hollywood used to come here in the forties and fifties. 'Wednesday was location day,' he says. 'Those old producers'd drive out here with a different young starlet every Wednesday afternoon. Scouting locations, they'd call it.'

'Has much changed?' Clara asks. Her accent cuts the air.

'Oh, I shouldn't think so,' Martin says calmly.

'Well, we don't arrest too many Hollywood producers here,' says the younger cop, grinning at Martin, and the older one, as if he's delivered the line before, is saying, 'I go back so far I can remember when we didn't even know what *marijuana* looked like.' But Clara is still watching Martin preening himself in the role of real

48

film producer. She is trying to read in his confident, treacherous features some hint of the person who existed a day and a half before in room 612 of the Century Plaza Hotel (on the old Century City lot!) and ignores the sergeants and the highway behind them. So while she turns at the pinched squeal of brakes and the inevitable thud, she has missed the young Latin driver — more anxious to leave the motel and the vicinity of police than you would guess from his round, enigmatic cheeks — accelerating too fast around the Oldsmobile and crew, and spinning out wide on to the highway. The station-wagon that swerved desperately around his pickup truck into the path of the approaching bus was also out of her line of vision.

NOW the blonde woman's hair is wet. She is parading along the driveway past Clara, fidgeting with the front of her bathrobe and murmuring, 'Poor Momma, Momma's got wet hair.'

'Yes,' Clara agrees, trying to catch her eye this time. Of course, the time elapsed, the experience shared, should be acknowledged. 'It's so *hot*,' Clara says to her.

Startled, the woman veers away from her across the driveway towards the black men in the directors' chairs. She tosses her dripping hair, tugs the bathrobe across her breasts and announces defiantly, 'It gets hot, Momma has to take a shower!'

The sun is setting on the cancelled shoot. In the rusty twilight all transactions at the motel are postponed. Although the paramedics have left with the body of the dead station-wagon driver and ferried away the concussed bus driver and four lacerated passengers, the driveway entrance is still blocked by police vehicles, their roof lights spinning. Traffic patrolmen much grimmer than the filmic sergeants are taking down witnesses' reports. From the tone of their questioning, Martin, in the absence of the young Latin speedster, is being made to feel the person most culpable for the fatal disarray. He is astonished that the police are focusing their attention on the crew and the Oldsmobile. They aren't interested in the black men and their transactions or the identity of the young Latin driver; they want to talk to the producer, the man in charge of this circus, on the hazards of a foreign film crew and a 1958-model car abutting the highway. In his anxiety Martin is faking a clipped British calmness. His politeness is excruciating. He excuses himself to call the British consulate, the production company in London, the advertising agency, the client, the insurance company and the man who rented out the Oldsmobile. 'I'm not sure where we stand at the moment,' he tells them all, nonchalantly pouring quarters into the motel's pay-phone. 'I'll get back to you ASAP.'

Clara is amazed at this impassive pretence. And, abruptly, at herself. She would warm to a show of nerves. Yes, he was also strangely calm at the Los Abrigados Hotel in Sedona, Arizona as the sunlight rose over the mesas and buttes into her room. She had never before seen the beauty in rock and desert, in the red silence of the hinterland. Suddenly she saw why Americans got carried away, and why they called it the 'heartland'. Later that morning one of the extras, a young Navajo woman, told her that she lived in Sedona 'because of the metaphysics'. So that was how the modern Indian put into words the mystical attachment to the land. 'The metaphysics are favorable,' the woman, Darlene Manygoats, told her, her eyes, too, glancing off to the side of Clara. Darlene had the dignity and noble cheekbones of a statue. 'I know what you mean,' Clara told her, but she was thinking more of context, remembering his certitude and calmness two hours before in the early desert light.

The metaphysics of Sun Valley were unfavorable, it was as simple as that. Clara paces the driveway again, like a prisoner in an exercise yard, her boundaries determined on one side by the men muttering on their chairs, on the other by the police barriers and lights and confusion. Behind the motel, between the two groups of milling men, a broken Cyclone fence cuts off a dusty half-acre of clay and weeds and litter. Clara climbs over it and heads toward the pool.

The shape of a fish. In a shopping arcade at the Los Abrigados with Martin she bought a wooden fish carved by Indians; its body, fins and tail were painted with many faces of the moon, smiling, frowning, grimacing, in all its phases. In England, middle-aged churchwardens had fish-shaped bumper stickers on their Austins. Peter the Fisherman, Saint Peter. This car is being driven by a middle-class, Tory-voting Christian. Clara stands by the pool's tail; there is just enough light to see that the head is the deep end. A metal ladder is still set halfway along the length, and Clara climbs down it into the pool. Cans and cardboard, bottles and rags scrape her; the bottom still slopes sharply, and underneath the rubbish the tiles are cracked and slippery. Were the metaphysics favorable here when Gene Underwood banked on his

51

vision? When hopeful starlets gambolled and splashed and sly old producers smoked post-coital cigars down at the shallow end?

Weren't the metaphysics always a little convoluted? Back in Sedona, Darlene Manygoats had a college degree but played Indians in TV commercials. She said that times were tough in Arizona, as elsewhere. Darlene's father and uncle were out on bail for poaching bald eagles. On top of those mesas and buttes they trapped the national symbol to make Indian head-dresses and artifacts. They were Indians — or, these days, Native Americans; the birds were under federal protection. Even serene Darlene thought several aspects of this state of affairs were ironic.

Now Clara stands in the head of the fish, in the dark, leaning back against the slope. The rear motel cabins effectively block off the lights from the highway, the crew and the police barriers. Just an obliquely angled TEL of the motel sign is visible, a pink mist in the sky, and the glow of the black men's cigarettes back in the turning circle. The noise is lower and disco music leaks from a far room.

So Jane is going to dance her tits off tonight? All of a sudden, strangely, Clara could almost dance herself. If they ever got back to town. Back to LA, the Century Plaza, back to London, back to Melbourne. Standing in the fish, she now hears a woman's high cry, near and snapped off, and a lower moan. Some animal yelps in the distance. She feels it is a coyote. This morning's *LA Times* had an article on the urban coyote problem. Coyotes were descending on Beverly Hills by night to gorge on discarded Big Macs and domestic pets. (Scientific examination of their droppings showed an increasing ability to digest Styrofoam.) Clara wants badly for it to be a coyote — and she wants the vague risk of it coming closer. She holds her breath and listens intently for another howl. Above her, at the side of the pool, there is, instead, a loose cough.

The shock it gives her astonishes her further. For seconds she is stunned. While still immobile, for some half-remembered reason, she says, 'Martin?'

'You taking a swim, babe?' asks the voice, and chuckles.

She has to shuffle uphill on the tiles and their shifting carpet of junk. The man is standing by the ladder. 'Hope you had a refreshing dip.' He is a dark mound peering down at her with the air on his teeth. 'No one but scorpions and rats had a refreshing dip here in twenty years.'

If the intention of the statement was to make her hurry, slide, stumble, it doesn't work. Every millimetre of her skin and scalp tingles, but she picks her feet up carefully and moves to the side. At the foot of the ladder she mutters some nonsense about filling in time. 'Just waiting to give evidence to the *police* out there,' she tells him. 'About the *accident*,' she stresses. Notwithstanding her fear she is unhappy with herself. This is too disordered. When she climbs out of the fish will the risk be greater or less? Does she want the howl nearer or further away? Or does she want the howl but not the coyote?

He grunts. 'Thought you might be looking for *company* out here. Out here in the dark in the old *swimming* pool.' He chuckles again but this laugh is higher, lamer, already resigned to disappointment or reality.

Even trembling she has to climb the ladder up to

him. It's amazingly steep and narrow and suddenly his arm blocks the way, hanging heavily down in her face. He smells like the clothes in the hotel wardrobe. He is offering her his hand! His hand is like a pad, a cushion which envelops hers and hoists her from the pool.

'Good *night*, police witness,' he says, stepping abruptly around her and rolling away toward the motel. He moves like an old man. She hears his grunt as he climbs over the fence.

Clara makes no pretence of sauntering back to the motel. As she hurries across the lot and over the fence she hears the giggles of his friends in the turning circle as the man from the pool rejoins them. But she doesn't look around, nor is she even slightly diverted by the police and crew as she reaches the motel. The music is louder here. In the motel room Stuart is watching a game show and drinking bourbon, and when she sees this, Clara's actions are even more decisive.

She has already shut the door, drawn the smoky curtains and turned down the TV. She has drunk from the bourbon bottle and smoked the dope. How perfect the room smells! There are cigars here and perfume, sweat and bank notes. The bedspread glows like a sunset in the desert. She inhales again — yes, semen. Blood!

'Oh, do the voice,' she asks now, lowering hers and smiling as she reaches across to touch Stuart the actor. 'Be American!'

MANDALAY

ONE July Sunday on Bondi beach after a storm, Philip Wardle makes a discovery. He is poking along the beach with his three daughters, the southerly in their hair, when he finds a citizenship card, coated in protective plastic, lying on the high-water mark among strands of kelp and the dry tentacle-strings of dead bluebottles. Thanks to its plastic cover it is still legible.

'This is to certify,' it proclaims, 'that Anna Luisa Sanchez, born in Bombay, India, in 1965, is an Australian citizen.' Her signature, slightly smeared, is on the bottom of the card.

Philip hadn't realised such things existed. A small card, about eight centimetres square, it seems designed to fit into a purse or pocket; to be produced, presumably, as some sort of *bona fide*. Turning the card over in his fingers he is disappointed it doesn't carry the owner's photograph.

He immediately feels he's holding something intensely personal, an item more intimate than a bank statement or even a love letter. His possession of the card is both an intrusion and a responsibility. Philip is what is called an intellectual-property lawyer, specialising in copyright, patents, licensing, trademarks, designs, trade secrets and practices. It doesn't take much imagination to guess that the owner of the card, this young woman of perhaps Portuguese-Goanese extraction (her name is a clue here), is dark-skinned or otherwise non-European in appearance, and that this could disadvantage her in her adopted country. It's important to her to be able to prove she is a citizen, so she takes the card everywhere with her — even to the beach.

LIKE some of his legal colleagues, Philip finds the beach has a calming effect on him. He uses it to relieve his tensions. It soothes him to surf and sunbake, to saunter along the shore or just to flop on the sand and lose himself in the rhythmic pattern of the breakers.

A secret: he envies the joggers whose never-ending procession along the beach-front leads to Tamarama and Bronte and beyond, to wiry muscles, lower blood pressure and reclaimed youth. He plans to join them any day now, even mimics them in his weekend tracksuit and road-hugging Nikes. But the squeaks of their soles on the promenade mock his extra ten kilos, his quasi-healthy presentation, and make him too self-conscious to begin seriously.

It's not his age they seem to scorn (half these fellows are older and greyer), but his cosy executive wrappings, his bodily comfort, while they turn out each increasingly chilly weekend (like Tony Warren from the Firm) in ever skimpier silk running shorts and singlets nonchalantly flaunting the names of famous marathons.

Warren, looking lean and sharp, manages to pound

past him every Sunday. Warren always has an over-the-shoulder quip and an amused wink. The wink gets Philip's goat, that and Warren's well-defined and displayed muscles. Warren is a Partner who has established a rapidly expanding national and international practice. Warren has a few years on him but his manner says, move aside old-timer. At the boardroom watering-hole on Friday nights Warren sips mineral water and hints at a vigorous sex life.

They've got Philip wrong, these beach athletes. He appreciates the spartan pleasures. He too likes Bondi in winter, actually preferring it to those Christmas-New Year holidays with their crowds of oiled narcissists, beach pollution and parking problems. In winter the water is clearer and cleaner. The light is softer. A stroll along the beach to get his blood moving, a quick swim and back into his tracksuit for a cup of espresso at Gianni's — this is his Sunday morning routine.

But temperate well-being is far from Philip's condition this morning. His marriage is becoming uneasy and events are beginning to create their own momentum and inevitability. He feels that things are slipping away. Even the familiar outing at Bondi with his daughters is already assuming the melancholy he foresees as marking, for him, the rest of their childhood.

This morning a milky light is throwing the headlands into sharp relief, accentuating the silhouettes of the other beachgoers and layering them with an unreal dimension. In the cold shallows a gaunt bearded man in saggy underpants, and a hugely pregnant woman, her belly and breasts bare, are rubbing themselves with kelp. She scrapes branches of leathery weed over and around her swellings, while he vigorously massages

59

his head and face with more spiky handfuls; now and then their intense ministrations overbalance them in the waves. Jane's pregnancies seem a lifetime ago: the morning sickness, the swollen ankles, the fainting in David Jones. He was on tenterhooks each time and treated her gingerly. This blue-veined sea-woman, presently receiving a necklace of sea-grapes from her crazed partner, could be another species.

Nudging each other, smothering giggles, his daughters speed across the sand. The weird light and the pale hair blowing across their faces obliterates their features. Behind them, Philip plods through the sand-crust, visualising their future only as *Sunday at Bondi*, a weekly bitter-sweet tableau in which this vague avuncular figure applies sun-tan cream, pushes swings, buys ice creams and says goodbye.

Then Megan jolts this slow-motion sepia mood. Her bare feet making indignant peep-peeps in the sand, she races over and thrusts out her hand. This plump and innocent starfish holds two used syringes. 'Hey, look!' she says. 'Junkies' blood!'

Anger, fear, disgust rush into his throat. What holds more emotional power than a needle in the palm of a six-year-old? Two of them. 'Did they prick you?' In a panic he checks her hand, then thankfully, gingerly, carries the needles to a garbage bin. He is too disturbed to discuss them, but Megan doesn't have any questions anyway. By the time he returns they're all playing happily; Susan has arranged a game of French skipping. At twelve an efficient organiser, she has the younger ones standing like posts in the sand, the elastic looped around their legs while she jumps it.

In front of the beach pavilion a tourist bus has just

drawn up, and forty or fifty Japanese honeymooners in immaculate casualwear climb down, sight the activity and begin scurrying together towards the girls. At first they tread the sand in measured portions, then, awkwardly removing their shoes and pulling cameras from cases, they fan out across the sand.

They reach the girls and surround them. Pink-faced, Susan jumps on. The idea of the game is to raise the height of the elastic and increase the difficulty; with each rise in height a general murmur goes out: 'Ahhh!' Some of the Japanese drop urgently on to one knee like intrepid war photographers to snap this indigenous action. Others encircle the self-conscious children and with encouraging mute gestures try to arouse them to even more photogenic antics. But all this concentrated attention, the increasing numbers of Japanese, makes Susan, now deeply red, trip on the elastic and stop. Megan stands agog. And Jennifer, the five-year-old, bursts into tears.

Philip sees the mortification of the honeymooners, steps into the ring of photographers and takes Jennifer's hand. There are embarrassed smiles and soft murmurs. Suddenly the photographers pretend to photograph the sea, or each other against it, and in a moment they have melted away.

The girls and he stroll down to the shore. And then he finds the citizenship card.

Anna Luisa Sanchez. He has always liked the name Anna. He thinks it womanly, exotic, erotic. Anna Karenina. Anna Magnani. Anna Sanchez. He doesn't need a picture. She is slim and attractive. He sees her hair, eyes, teeth. Sadly, the loss of her card has changed her usual vivacity into a frown of anxiety. She

61

is wringing her sensual, finely boned hands (with their long tapered red nails) and summoning up the courage to explain the loss to boorish bureaucrats. Oh, Anna, pacing the shore in your wave-lashed sari, the southerly whipping your long loose hair, searching for the proof of your identity!

Not that she lacks steel, or fire. But she is single, with no one to turn to, in a foreign country. Those slender arms, that glimpse of brown skin at the side of the waist, the small of the back, between the sari's folds. The Karma Sutra fingernails! Philip holds the proof of her identity in his hands. It's suddenly as if he's in control of Anna Sanchez.

The cold rises through the seat of his tracksuit as Philip sits on the sand fingering the card and relishing this sneaky sense of power. A chance insight into a stranger's life is an intriguing thing. Strange how these insights are happening more often lately. Maybe when one door is closing others open just a crack. Only three days before there was that discovery at the Firm's annual dinner: the tightness of his old dinner suit had led him into two new lives.

At the last moment he had to hire a dinner suit for the dinner, and was abruptly introduced into the wedding party of a young couple. He can remember their names: Belinda and Jim. He found Jim's speech notes in the inside jacket pocket, jotted on an index card, the ink slightly runny from the dry-cleaning. ('All credit to the bridesmaids, Julie and Libby, who look extremely attractive . . .') And another card tied with white ribbon announcing something like, 'Belinda and Jim, 27th May, 1989' above a romantic illustration of a church.

(Also in the pocket was a terse reminder card from the suit-rental company warning that late returns incurred a fine of $15 a day.)

Although he was sitting next to Bronwyn North-cott, wife of the youngest Partner, he paid little attention either to her or the speeches. He was watching Jane sitting next to Tony Warren. Jane was laughing with her head thrown back. Often she touched Warren's arm to stress her conversational points, or tipped the side of her head against his shoulder. Her own shoulders were bare and confident. In the light of the hotel's banquet room her shoulders gleamed. He recognised them but they looked unfamiliar. Because Jane is very lively on social occasions he knows people imagine, wrongly, that she is like that at home.

At least the wine was good and plentiful. He leaned back in his chair and imagined the suit's previous outing — young Jim, his fellow 42 Regular, flushed with champagne and good humor, beaming at his bride, fulsome with praise of Libby and Julie; Jim dashing and handsome in their mutual cloth; the bridesmaids pretty and giggly. (The ink was faint and watery but he thought Jim had also reminded himself to compliment Libby and Julie on their 'radiance'.) Some of Jim's friends had their eyes on Libby and Julie, if he wasn't mistaken — and vice versa. For some reason he pictured Libby in particular letting her hair down at the wedding.

On Thursday night he envied Jim. But, drinking wine, he felt affection for the whole bridal party. He put Jim's speech notes back in the jacket pocket. Perhaps the next bridegroom or company slave might draw emotional sustenance from them.

When the dinner ended Jane drove them home. The trip passed in silence.

IN the car now, licking a gelato, Susan announces, 'I'm really down on junkies. I'll never go out with a drug addict when I'm fourteen or so.'

'Me either,' Megan says. 'Re-pul-sive.'

Philip's heart leaps. 'They're sick,' he says. Rumor has it that kids are popping pills at the girls' school these days. Private schools are supposed to be a guarantee against that! What's happening? Those late-sixties parties with a wine flagon and an elaborately shared joint could be a hundred years ago. The precious air of ceremony, the ambiguous odour of sanctity and sin, the raunchy idealism, the camaraderie of the shared spittle, seem as ludicrously cute as flappers and bathtub gin. Big Brother and the Holding Company, Jefferson Airplane, Country Joe and the Fish. Whatever happened to Country Joe when the war ended? Philip turns around in the driver's seat. 'Susan, I want you to tell me if any kid offers you anything.'

Anna Sanchez's card is in his tracksuit pocket. Perhaps he was going to show it to Jane, but when they get home she isn't there. There's a note stuck to the fridge by a magnetised plastic fried-egg: 'Back about 1.30. Make yourselves a sandwich.' Jane has recently taken up her old calling, physiotherapy — on Sundays dropping in at her consulting rooms to redecorate or catch up on bookwork. He believes she is consciously distancing herself from him, gradually widening the space until they are separated altogether. At dinner parties he feels she gives away more than is required, even by Eastern Suburbs hostesses. She says, 'Thank God I've found myself again.' She chatters about her patients. She is proud to be treating the injuries of some well-known sportsmen, including the knee of a West Indian cricketer. Other women, he has noticed, respond to this insider physical news with a keen risqué interest.

'Whatever happened to professional ethics?' he interrupted one of these conversations, slightly drunk, one Saturday night. 'The old Hippocratic oath?' On his face he could feel a fierce smile.

'That's doctors,' Jane said, airily waving her wine glass. 'We're allowed to gossip. And anyway, it's only a bloody *hamstring*.'

The Sunday before last he called unexpectedly at her consulting rooms with her spare keys, an excuse at the ready — did she need a hand with anything? Actually, he was becoming suspicious of these Sunday absences. He anticipated the worst; he also prayed for this not to be happening. In the Volvo he arrived as silently as a spy. The brass plate carried her maiden name. The beginning of the end, he thought. But part of him admired the polished professionalism this represented and was paternally proud.

The front office was empty: the *Vogues* and *Times* sat in their precise stacks. An intruder in the unfamiliar atmosphere, Philip padded through these feminine yet workmanlike premises. Of the person he knew there was hardly a trace. In her office, on her desk, was a framed photograph of four strangers, Jane and the girls. And there, on her examination bench, lay Jane — neatly, even rigidly, asleep. She was dressed in her

65

weekend jeans and sweater, her hands lightly crossed on her stomach, breathing through her mouth.

He stood in her territory, his heart beating fast, for several minutes. Even from the doorway he could hear every breath. He considered the action of kissing her, but not the possibility. He couldn't bare to face a startled stranger. Suddenly a shy voyeur, he crept out and drove home.

IN his office next morning Philip hunts up Sanchezes in the phone book. There are forty-eight of them. There are, however, only three A. Sanchezes, and one is a Bondi listing.

He picks up the phone. Anna's card is on the desk. Not for twenty-five years has he felt so nervous. Old school-dance invitations swim in his head; edgy dates, his own fake-cool voice. At sixteen he was a martyr to love. He takes a deep breath and has dialled most of the number when his secretary walks in. He hangs up at once and covers the card with his hand.

'Is there a number you want, Mr Wardle?'

'No, thank you,' he says.

He has important litigation matters at hand but he is too distracted to concentrate. Dates, names, precedents slide quickly out of mind. For once he eats a sandwich at his desk. His office overlooks Hyde Park; below him stenographers and clerks enjoy lunch on the grass. Boys and girls canoodle in the winter sun. Philip can smell the stenographers' perfume, taste their sweet diet-cola lips.

By four he is resolved. He leaves the office, gets his car and drives to Bondi. The afternoon is sunny but crisp. Long shadows fall across Bondi Road, and the flow of traffic, random and edgy, keeps him on the verge of an accident. At an intersection a tattooed boy, grinning inanely, walks against the lights and almost under the Volvo's wheels. A block further and a taxi spins out of a petrol station in front of him, the driver answering his complaining horn with an aggressive finger. Despite the mild temperature Philip's scalp is sweating.

Up the hill from the sea he stops outside a three-storeyed block of flats. On its stucco facade the name *Mandalay* stands out in concrete letters, and around its mail boxes junk-mail and old newspapers unfurl and flutter in the breeze. His senses are so acute he can smell the damp newsprint; the paper smells humid, almost seminal. Against a fence post a motorbike is tethered with a heavy chain. Not so much for reassurance as proof of entrée, Philip pats the card in his pocket.

The phone book gave only the street address. He begins his search at a ground floor flat. Holding the card at the ready like a charity collector, he knocks on the door. Nothing. Loud pop music draws him around the back of the building. On a staircase in the sun two Maoris and a thin youth with a night person's complexion sit by a radio smoking and drinking beer. A toddler lurches up the stairs between their legs. Below them, a red-haired girl in tight jeans and sheepskin boots hangs washing on a clothes hoist. The glances they all give Philip's grooming, age and suit are neutral and impassive, an apt reception for landlords. The girl turns her back on him at once; one buttock of her jeans has a smily face-patch.

67

He is forced to climb five or six stairs to proffer the card.

'Excuse me, does this lady live here?'

His slightly breathless voice hangs over the scrappy back yard, too smooth and educated. A smell like burnt fish is coming from the next landing. The men slowly take the card and pass it between them without expression or comment. He senses that their presumptions have changed: more Immigration Department than landlord. Authority, bureaucracy, trouble. They shrug, hawk and cough, drag on cigarettes and beer cans. Running out of props, one of the Maoris, fleshy and short, with a 1960s hairstyle like an Apache's, says, finally, 'Don't know, mate.' His mouth reveals bare gums. Loud vapid music swamps even this reply. One of the others, maybe the sallow boy, belches behind him. The belch is more than gas; it's a statement of boredom and defiance, a ruffling of scrawny rooster feathers. It's a territorial belch.

Philip goes back one step. 'She's probably needing this card,' he says. 'I just found it. She's probably a bit lost without it.'

'Couldn't say, mate,' says the toothless Maori.

Wrong-footed on the staircase, Philip looks towards the girl for support. But she has spun the clothes hoist around so she is hidden by a sheet. Her boots show underneath. The child bumping down the steps on its bottom has her red hair.

Another, louder, belch sounds behind him.

What can he do but leave? A snort, perhaps of laughter, follows him around the front of the building. As he reaches the street the early setting sun is in his eyes. A boy on a skateboard rumbles past him; above, to the west, a police helicopter clatters against the sun. Grey clouds turn pink over the coastal plain. As he moves to the car, the Pacific rolls before him and settles in the softer eastern light. On the headlands a rosy mist blurs the menacing lines of the apartment blocks and plays over the red suburban roofs.

He is moved by this strangely Mediterranean, North African beauty. Why did he feel so romantic? He wishes he could share this light and this calm evening ocean. He is surprised to feel so calm. He feels empty, but at least the pressure is off. At least he is released from the tension of hope. To be honest, it is not quite impossible with Jane. It is not yet too late.

The sunset is still in his eyes as he gets into the car, turns the key in the ignition — yes, the sunset — but was that a flicker at *Mandalay*'s upstairs window? Did he see a flash of dark hair behind the curtains? A glittering eye? A swirl of silk?

Philip's neck throbs against his collar; his chest jumps. He is out of the car, hurrying back to the flats and up two flights of stairs. His exhilaration easily shuts out the pop music and burnt fish. There is no answer to his knock, but he expects this reaction and is not at all put off. On the contrary, there are now set routines to follow. Mannered guidelines. An orderliness is proper in an affair of such rare spirituality. He takes several deep breaths before sliding her property under the door. Then, for her, he leaves his own spoor, his escutcheon, his caste mark. He leaves his business card.

RIVER WATER

THE dogs spring out from the shade under the water tanks when Rita lifts the gate latch. They lunge to the limit of their chains but she steps carefully outside their radius of frenzy and heads for the welfare office.

At the noise Mrs Beckwith steps warily out of the office — which is just a section of veranda closed off with fibro-cement from the officer's residence — frowning and tapping a pen against her teeth. 'Mr Beckwith's in town,' she says, and repeats herself, louder, over the barking. She is wearing a loose sundress, but she still looks hot, and various straps and bows bite into her freckled shoulders. 'Police business.'

Rita pauses between the loquat tree and the bottom step. The dogs grumble behind her, then slump down and sigh in the dust. Rita didn't expect this sweating wife, this unhappy hot triangle. This woman should be down south, typing in an air-conditioned office with twenty others. In charge of the tea and biscuits and the engagement present collections. Rita's thoughts are sympathetic, not derisory; she once dreamed of such a job herself and, for six months, had one. Back with the shire council in sixty-six. Before Lexie.

Mrs Beckwith is looking at her impatiently, sucking

her pen. It dawns on Rita that she hasn't actually spoken to Mrs Beckwith yet; she is happy and feeling friendly towards her, but she hasn't said anything to her. So she says, 'No worries, Mrs Beckwith,' and a wave of pleasurable anticipation makes her limbs jumpy. She bends down and picks up a fallen loquat and flips out the seed with her thumbnail. 'Just called in to tell Mr Beckwith everything's fixed.' She smiles up at the white woman. 'My cousin Charlie's coming with his truck tomorrow, give us a hand to move.'

Mrs Beckwith nods, hitches a strap.

And now Rita can't stop talking. 'He's been dog-baiting and fencing, Charlie, out Talthorpe way for the Barretts. Bad year for dingoes out there, Mrs Beckwith, out Talthorpe way, Ironwood, out west ...'

'Yes. Well, Mr Beckwith will be back this afternoon.'

Rita waves a jaunty arm. 'No worries.' Nothing can bring her down this morning. She is preparing to close the conversation, even to say goodbye, swivelling in the dust at the bottom of the steps, an eye anticipating the dogs, when she asks suddenly, 'What police business, Mrs Beckwith?'

The woman is already moving inside. She pokes her head out again. 'The Gary Mappsett business.' The screen door slaps shut.

Rita detours around the dogs and out the gate. Even at this end of the settlement, away from the shacks, she can hear Mappsetts yelling, glass breaking. She decides to take the long way home, around the south end of the settlement by the river. She closes her ears to the Mappsetts. She has had twenty-two years of Mappsetts. Mappsetts and Shaws and Burnses and

74

Bulgongs and no drainage and the smell of pit lavatories always in the house.

Nothing much has changed since Lexie brought her here in sixty-six. That day it seemed far more than thirty kilometres from the last town — flat red plains in all directions, and one wrong-looking tree breaking the horizon. Relentless red dirt, dusty *and* swampy — that took some doing; perfect for both brown snakes and mosquitoes. And the river cutting through the dirt, buckling and twisting in on itself like one of its own blind eels.

'Good fishing, anyway,' Lexie said weakly (and inaccurately, it turned out, once the cotton-spraying started upriver). He became quiet as the settlement appeared: the two dozen board-and-tin shacks poking abruptly out of the earth, the car bodies, the garbage heaps. She climbed out of Lexie's uncle's truck and the lavatory smell hit her and a couple of drunk Mappsett men skittered over and Lorna Mappsett was on the doorstep to greet her.

'I know your auntie,' Lorna said, and gave her a housewarming present, a wall plaque in plaster-of-Paris which announced *God is Our Refuge and Strength, A Very Present Help in Trouble*. 'It belonged to the old chap who lived here,' Lorna said. 'Poor old Tommy Bulgong kicked off a month ago.' She gestured vaguely. 'He's buried in the back yard.'

Rita's arms were full of belongings. She'd had a hope-chest: sheets, towels, table cloths, lace doilies. *A dead man in the back yard.* Planted there on the step, Lorna was a stolid barrier between her and her new house. Lexie was shifting his feet, dying to take off his boots and lay the dust. Not only the dust. 'Thank you, auntie,' he said. Then, shy and proud, he declared, 'Rita worked for the council. In the rates office. A town girl,' he said unnecessarily.

'Long way from home, here,' Lorna said. Children and puppies were swarming around her. She blinked into the sun, closing first one cloudy eye and then the other, never keeping both open at once. She stood on Rita's rickety honeymoon porch, steadfastly one-eyed, patting children and puppies and slowly shooing the flies from her eyes.

VARIOUS Mappsetts are still screaming around the shacks — Rita can hear one of them banging on an oil drum or something — so she sits down by the river until the din stops. It's a school day, but a small crowd of children, three or four Burnses and some of the Bulgong girls, are playing in the river. A baby stroller is perched on the slick crest of the bank. In it sits one of the Burns babies, picking its nose and watching the frolics. One more inch, a vigorous wriggle, and the stroller will speed down the bank into the river.

Rita slithers along the bank to the baby. She drags the stroller back from the brink. Now the baby can't see the fun, and bursts into tears. Rita could slap it, she's suddenly so furious. 'You kids down there!' she yells. 'You Burns kids — Donny, Shane. You, too, Marion. You want your little brother drowned and eaten by yabbies like Richie Shaw? Get up here and take this baby home!'

Her voice is still shrill in her ears as she sits down

again. Two kids, sodden shorts drooping down their legs, scramble up the bank, big-eyed and half-laughing. The smaller one dives into the stroller on top of the protesting baby, and the bigger boy wheels them off. A giggle floats back in the dust. *Fat arse.*

'I'll smack yours for you!' Rita shouts after them. Their quick spindly legs seem hardly to touch the ground. 'You should be in school!' Those Burns kids are getting as wild as the Mappsetts, thirty or forty terrors in each family, and more coming all the time.

Like she told the residents' meeting, standing up to Mr Beckwith: 'I've been trying for twenty years to get out of here. I count myself lucky my six kids only have to sleep two to a bed. Some of the others (Mappsetts, Shaws, Burnses, she could have told him) are in a terrible way. Five kids to a bed, all sexes and sizes. It's wicked, some of these houses.'

Lorna Mappsett had forty-one living in her shack — her five sons' and two daughters' families — but she sat there in the schoolroom (the young school teacher, Mr Kennett, was on-side), blinking sideways up at the blackboard and not saying a word to Mr Beckwith. Not saying boo, even though she had to sleep in her kitchen with a daughter and five grandchildren, and the rest crammed into the other two rooms or sleeping outside. Not talking, not even voting for the 'renovation or relocation' request like everyone else.

It wasn't as if the chance looked likely to crop up again. Mr Beckwith couldn't get over the surprise of them calling a residents' meeting at all (and the school-room being made available for it). He'd agreed to it only because he thought it was about the floods and the broken pump. It took the double calamity to nudge him into acting for once without departmental instructions from Sydney.

When he told them that the problem of the broken pump, which had brought river water to each shack since 1938 (or, to be precise, to the single tap in each shack's outside wash-house), would be looked into by an engineer coming up from Tamworth any day now, and that bore water for drinking would be trucked in from Toonabilla by Thursday, his smile said that's the end of that. His smile said, see, if you co-operate you get things. (His smile managed to exclude Mr Kennett, that interfering bearded 'outsider'.) It said, otherwise, well, the department controls things like firewood, transport to town, unemployment benefits. Water.

And then she, Rita, drawing on six weeks' experience in the shire council office in 1966, before Lexie, raised her hand and said, 'Excuse me, I move that we ask the department to provide us with rain-water tanks, and that the settlement be fixed up.'

Mr Beckwith stared at her.

'I further move,' she said, gathering momentum, 'that when the money is allocated, it's spent to build new houses. Either here for those who want to stay, or in nearby towns for those who want to leave.'

Mr Beckwith said nothing.

'Anyone like to second that?' invited Mr Kennett, looking around happily.

'I'm game,' said Ruby Bulgong, who had two kids in hospital with 'the gastric' again. 'They can bulldoze my place into the river tomorrow.'

Except for Lorna Mappsett, sitting on her hands and squinting up at the educational charts on the walls —

the basic food groups and popular sports of Australia — the motion was carried unanimously.

LAST week dead cattle and bush animals were floating down this river and now they're playing in it. Drinking it. As far as Rita knows the river water has never been tested, even before the floods. They add chlorine to it before it's pumped to the wash-houses (when the pump is working), but that doesn't clean out the mud and rotting plants and mosquito larvae.

Water brown as Bundaberg rum. Lexie put rum in it, too, to kill the germs, he said. No cheap wine for Lexie. On the Morgans' station the white stockmen drank Bundaberg rum every night, Lexie and the boys only when they were off the property. (One drink for them and they were fired; it made Bundy rum very desirable.) When Lexie came home the Mappsett boys would be hanging around all day, calling out for a bottle of his Bundy. And at night the sweet rum sweat coming out his pores. The kids asleep and Lexie's smell of skin and breath filling the shack in a cloud.

Sitting here on the river bank she can still cry for Lexie. Especially now with things working out for once.

THREE days ago who would have guessed at things working out? Not when the engineer from Tamworth drove off muttering about obsolete machinery and parts needed from Newcastle, and the bore water truck still hadn't arrived from Toonabilla, and everyone began raiding the welfare office's two rain-water tanks.

Openly, nothing sly about it. Everyone sending their kids over with buckets and flagons to get water. (She'd sent Craig and Gregory over herself.) It would have been demeaning to go themselves, to be seen taking the officer's water, so they sent the kids. And the kids kept leaving the taps running and wasting water and Beckwith brought in the dogs to guard the tanks.

When the women came to her she didn't know how to react. She felt nervous and proud. They'd always kept her just at arm's length. Lexie said it was because she was 'different skin', from another clan and language group. She didn't know anything about that, didn't want to know. She did know her reputation as the aloof townie, the sobersides, the prim housewife. The intermediary to the white man, it seemed now.

'Rita, tell this Beckwith he's gone too far,' Ruby Bulgong said, calling around with a packet of cream biscuits. 'Warn him we'll kick up a bloody fuss this time. No mistake, he'll find himself on the TV.'

Even Lorna Mappsett, padding into her kitchen behind Ruby, was steamed up. 'Your auntie and I was in tents at Goondiwindi before this place,' she said. 'I had five babies in tents. This is worse than tents.'

'You came up trumps last time,' Ruby said, working her way through the biscuits. 'You called his bluff, Rita, at the school.'

Lorna blinked furiously. 'We had no water problems at Goondiwindi. No water problems whatsoever.'

'All right,' Rita said.

Ruby patted her cheek and ate the remaining biscuit. On their way out the women's fingertips trailed

80

over her ornaments, her polished surfaces, in respect and wonder. They stopped in front of her photographs, the three framed studio portraits she'd had done in Toonabilla: one of the kids all together (the two big girls, Elizabeth and Catherine, sitting; the first boy, Craig, standing between them; the three youngest, Gregory, Margaret and Vincent — the Band-Aid just showing on his knee — kneeling in front); one of Lexie and her with the kids; and one of Lexie and her by themselves; everyone dressed up to the nines, clean clothes and new haircuts.

'Nice-looking boy, Lex,' Lorna said. 'Dreadful shame. Never mind, you got a few more babies in you yet, sweetie.'

'Mind them dogs, Reet,' Ruby said.

The dogs. With Mr Beckwith's unexpected help from the veranda, she'd safely circled them, keeping her eye on the yellow German Shepherd, as Mr Beckwith advised. ('He's vicious, that one. He'll go for you with his tail wagging.')

'Look at it my way,' Mr Beckwith said to her over a glass of lemon barley water on the veranda. He sat her in a canvas deckchair, trapped her there, with her seat dragging on the floor. Below them the dogs grunted and sighed. Parrakeets squabbled in the loquat tree. Mr Beckwith wore a snowy white vest and khaki shorts, like a little boy. Brown strappy sandals. He must have been past fifty. He pointed to the big wet patch on the ground. 'Fifteen hundred gallons of emergency water supplies run into the sand. My responsibility, Rita.'

He knew she understood the meaning of responsibility. He had only to look at the way she'd coped since

81

her husband's death, bringing up the children and so on. She was an example to the local Aboriginal people — and well they knew it!

Her savings, for one thing. He'd checked her building society account and noted the current balance: $785. Very impressive, the fact that she'd been saving since 1966. And just between them — he wouldn't want it to go any further — he took the point she'd made at the residents' meeting about relocation.

'A useful suggestion,' he said. The department wasn't insensitive to useful suggestions, he went on, smiling with his grey face. She tried to take her eyes off the white whiskers in the corners of his mouth, and his white shins. The afternoon was standing still. She could watch herself sitting back in the deckchair on the veranda, breathing strange air, picking up the glass of lemon barley water, admiring its clarity, sipping it. She heard raucous male laughter from the settlement, a woman's angry shouting, more laughter.

Mr Beckwith crossed his shining shins. 'We can advance you $215 to make up your deposit on a house in Toonabilla. The department has one house at its disposal.'

She didn't dare take in the overwhelming words. His deckchair scraped on the veranda. Parrakeets screeched. She raised the glass to her lips again, felt the last tangy drop go down, and kept the glass there, pretending to drink. Eventually she had to put it down.

He cleared his throat. 'A standard house, of course. Bungalow-style, three bedrooms, electricity and so forth. Sewered.' He hesitated, and looked to be considering a smile. 'Town water supply, naturally.'

*　　*　　*

THE hubbub is rising around the shacks, the tin-banging and shouting, but then car doors slam suddenly, and engines roar away, and soon the settlement is almost quiet. As Rita climbs the bank and sets off home she sees Bobby Mappsett's old Fairlane and two town taxis pelting along the track to the Toonabilla Road.

Police business. The Gary Mappsett business. She can easily guess the sequence of events: the cashing of the dole cheques, the drinking, the fighting, the arrest, the roughing up by police, the night in the lockup, the appearance in court, the shy plea of guilty (a different boy today, a scabby boy, dried blood on his face and scalp, on his swollen knuckles hanging over the dock rail), and automatic jail sentence. Three, six or nine months, depending on the property damage.

The old story. But now this infectious new stage, about to show itself again when three carloads of affronted Mappsetts, Burnses, Bulgongs and Shaws spilled into Toonabilla. She doesn't understand it. Frustration to her is the smell of pit-lavatories for twenty-two years. A fifty-year-old wood stove. Flood-waters under the baby's cot. Murky river water. When she aches it is for modern things, clean and ordered things, things that work properly. Hanging up the washing without a dead man under your feet.

This whipped-up disruption embarrasses her. It's too wild and muddled to grasp. What's the point in smashing the windows of the babywear shop, the florist's, the video hire? Where's the satisfaction? Where's the sense or profit or even the politics in it?

It's like someone throwing a switch. An electric shock. One minute they're playing cards, kicking a football, drinking, snoozing, joking. Suddenly news arrives, borne on the air somehow, and they're throwing rocks, tearing pickets off fences for weapons, screaming like crazy men. This is new behaviour to Rita, but maybe disturbingly old. Is this screeching destruction what *tribal* was like?

Approaching the shacks, she tells herself none of this matters any more. Not this broken glass in her yard, not this (her heart jumps) garbage strewn on her porch, not (steadying herself on the door jamb) the urine puddles on the doorstep or the phlegm inching down the windows.

We're leaving. Charlie will be here with the truck tomorrow. It can't worry her any longer, even though the moaning echo of the Mappsetts is staying with her, growing shrill and louder and forcing her finally to turn around.

The women are in her yard, wobbling toward her, entwined like caterpillars. Lorna is in front, wailing softly, held up by her daughters. They move through the glass and garbage and crowd on to the porch.

'Come back, did you?' calls Lorna. 'Oh, Rita, you surprised me, girl. A day of surprises.' She falls forward but is caught by the women.

'Got your house in town, we hear,' Ruby says. 'Not exactly what we thought you was organising, Rita. You and the department.'

The key won't fit into the lock. She needs to go inside and close the door and pack her things. Charlie is coming with the truck tomorrow and they have to be ready.

'We won't bother you,' Ruby says. 'Just give us something for Lorna, quieten her down. Bottle of

84

something strong. Sleeping pills maybe. She's got to have something, her boy hanged there in the police cells.'

Rita connects with the key and opens the door. The urine puddle has already spread inside. *Hanged?* She turns back to them.

Lorna is moaning. 'Not a moody boy, not a sad boy. Twenty years old.' She seems to fall, to trickle, through the women's hands on to the porch. Her substance is suddenly gone; they pick her up with difficulty. 'Why would my happy-go-lucky boy want to hang himself? He loved his football, his boxing. Wouldn't he be too drunk to tie knots in his sweatshirt, string himself up?' She doesn't blink; her eyes are oddly inset and piercing. *'Don't you think so, Rita?'*

There has been — is still — a bottle of Bundaberg rum, unopened, under the bed. Rita wipes the dust off it and hands it to Lorna.

RITA gets down the suitcase from the top of the wardrobe, sets it on the bed and sits beside it. The same bag she brought from town in sixty-six. Gradually, ordinary sounds begin to register again: dogs, birds, snatches of song from the school. Children singing 'Yellow Submarine'. Car engines in the distance. The engine noises stop, car doors slam, the dogs bark louder. Rita hurries to the window.

The menace of the phlegm-streaked glass stuns her for a moment. Her thoughts lose their order and she finds it hard to breathe. Then she squints through the smears down toward the welfare office. Mr Beckwith's car is back from town; a police car stands beside it. With things under control she takes a long breath and feels calmer.

Clean up. Rita goes into the kitchen and carries a bucket of the welfare office rain-water over to the stove. She lights a fire from kindling and lifts the bucket on to the stove. She is breathing easier. Charlie's coming with the truck tomorrow. When children's voices float in — *We all live in a yellow submarine, a yellow submarine* — she makes herself hum the song.

The kids will be home in an hour. She is thinking this, planning the right routine in her head, when heavy sober footsteps sound outside, pause, and crunch through the debris in the yard and on to the porch.

A man's voice says, 'Jesus!' and another man's voice warns, disgustedly, 'Watch your feet!' and they are at the door, banging on it, and their feet are scraping with impatience.

It's Mr Beckwith, in white shirt and long trousers today, taking no notice of her smile, with two cops glaring behind him. Mr Beckwith is wrinkling his nose at the stink of urine and garbage, but his expression is acquiring layers of confidence and relief by the second. When he speaks it's with the air of someone whose good nature may previously have been exploited but whose authority and commonsense are about to prevail.

He shakes his head sorrowfully. 'These premises are in a bad state, Rita. Most disappointing.'

She shakes her head, too, because she is incapable of speech. Even though he is frowning he doesn't look terribly displeased at the mess. There is a glimmer of something in his eye, something chilly and masculine.

'I suppose you've heard about the Gary Mappsett business?' Mr Beckwith doesn't wait for an answer. 'A sad business. I've just been to see old Lorna, offer my condolences, do what I can to help.'

She can just nod. Her senses are spinning with the urine smell, the embarrassment and dread. The pungency of it all makes her weak. Abruptly, she speaks, very fast. 'The Mappsett boys did this. Messed up my place, all those wild young fellas. I'm going to clean it up quick-smart.'

He agrees briskly, not looking at her, vaguely eyeing the mess. 'Rita,' he announces, 'the department has a new policy on these suicides in custody. We don't wait around for the inquests and so forth to decide there's been a particular stressful situation.' He turns and fixes her with a serious look. 'We act immediately to alleviate the family's situation.'

She is trying hard to deflect his words, to dodge them, before they turn into weapons. It would be nice to fill her head with a silly song, 'Yellow Submarine', kids' sweet voices, but the singing at the school has stopped. What is there to deaden the impact of his talking? She gazes around; one of the cops is stamping something off his boot, muttering under his breath; the other is staring upwards, away from all this, up at the sky. So she looks up, too. Perfectly clear. No rain coming.

Gary Mappsett's suicide, Mr Beckwith is saying solemnly, has drawn the department's attention to the overcrowding at the Mappsett cottage. 'I've just been there and seen the situation myself.'

She can hear herself murmur lamely, 'Won't take

87

me an hour to clean up this mess,' but it's too late, he's smiling tightly at her now, saying he's sure she understands the department's position, that the Mappsetts are a most unfortunate case, that he hopes she won't mind stepping aside for them.

Stepping aside?

'Of course you'll be put on the list for future relocation.'

The cop who was staring at the sky coughs just then, pointedly, and begins adjusting his belt. The foot-stamper gives a sort of determining snort. Mr Beckwith looks at her in a friendly way, the look he offered her on his veranda with the glass of lemon barley water. His hand flaps goodbye almost jauntily. 'Old Lorna deserves this.'

She watches them stroll away. The cops take off their hats, climb in their car and drive off; Mr Beckwith disappears into his office. She must sit down, lie down, have a drink. Oh, Lexie's Bundy rum. Lorna has the last bottle. The house *and* the bottle. Rita laughs, and cries. For Lexie, for the second time today. Lexie, who worked hard. Was never out of work. Who only drank off the property. Off-the-property meant the Morgans' last gate, however, and still three hundred kilometres to drive home. Three hundred kilometres and how many bottles of Bundy? With Norman Bulgong's body the way it was in the back seat, and the other three bodies thrown clear — Lexie's twenty metres from the wreckage — they couldn't even tell who was driving.

Even though she was just a Christmas drinker, a birthday drinker, a genteel port-and-lemonade drinker, she gave up alcohol altogether after the accident. Why not? It had killed Lexie. She couldn't look at a bottle without the sadness and anger flooding back. But now she needs a drink, anything at all, and she's on her knees in the wash-house, rummaging under the sink, in the tea-chest of Lexie's stuff that she can't bring herself to give away. Little spiders have got in already, a couple of earwigs, but she can smell rum, tantalisingly, because it is Lexie's smell, still on his shirts and jeans after six months, and it fills her head. But there is no rum, only the memory of it in the memory of Lexie's smooth, tired skin.

Rita straightens up. A stone is clattering on the roof. Another hits the tin and slides to the ground. There are hoots and cries in the front yard.

She runs through her house. Through the kitchen. The bucket is boiling on the stove: the boiling rain-water to clean up their filth. Rita grabs it, lifts it off the stove, paying no heed to the heat in her hands and against her body, and carries it to the door. When she throws open the door four or five youths are in the yard, reeling up to the porch. The Mappsett boys — for they are still boys, the youngest only thirteen or fourteen — begin to state their business, which is to call, in their grief and confusion, for another bottle of that Bundy rum. What stops them in their tracks is the sight of Rita on her doorstep, hoisting up the steaming bucket, swinging it back and screaming into the afternoon.

THE LAWYERS OF
AFRICA

MY son who speaks to me once or twice a year has been to Chad.

When he was young I didn't imagine he would grow up to be someone who travelled, without fuss, to Chad. But he goes to all those sorts of places — Guyana, Syria, Burma, Bolivia, Brunei. He buys native artifacts. He travels light. He seems to be always on call. I get the occasional laconic postcard, the note on hotel stationery.

I found myself discussing his travels the other night at the Wallaces. 'Andrew has just been to Chad,' I said. I don't think I got across the fact that as a boy Andrew was a timid kid who got homesick at weekend scout camps in the Blue Mountains. Or that his mother and I had not anticipated adventures. But no-one at the Wallaces had been to Chad or had anything to add on the subject.

'I wonder when he'll settle down,' Hilary Wallace said.

'Oh, well,' Frank Wallace said. He, too, gave Chad short shrift. It did serve, however, as an adequate opening for Frank. 'They have this zoo in Kuala Lumpur,' he went on quickly, 'which is *very* strange.'

We were sitting around the Wallaces' table after

dinner — Frank and Hilary, the Camerons, Eve and myself, with our brandies and ports and coffees. The Wallaces were just back from a holiday in Malaysia and keen to talk about it, time and their safe return having given the usual tropical idiosyncracies a humorous symmetry.

'They open this zoo only for the tourists,' Frank said. 'The locals are kept locked out.' He's as assertive and lively at the dinner table as he is in court, and he pushed back his chair at this point, stood up, leaned on the table and said, in a parody of an ingratiating Indian voice, 'But you can come right inside, sir and madam, and feast your eyes on our extensive range of wild beasts.'

Hilary dropped into the story from her end of the table. 'There was absolutely no-one else in the whole zoo. It was totally empty. Just us and this Sikh zoo keeper in a turban.'

At his end of the table, Frank spoke louder in his Indian voice and made bossy ushering motions. 'You can come *right* inside,' he said. 'So,' he continued in his normal voice, 'we went in and walked around, and it was your typical zoo, some gardens and cages and pits, a little smaller perhaps, the animals a bit more scrawny and furtive-looking.'

'And there was absolutely no-one else there,' Hilary added quickly. 'Not a soul.'

Frank glanced at her. 'And there was no-one else there,' he repeated. 'But it wasn't long before we got the feeling we were being followed.' Now he looked over his shoulder, shrugged and signified bemusement. He strode up and down the dining room, miming a zoo visitor who suspected he was being followed,

94

then suddenly turned, pointed and shouted, 'Ahah!'

'And there,' Frank quickly hunched his body and let his arms dangle loosely in front of him, 'was this funny-looking ape following us.'

'Everywhere we went,' Hilary said.

Frank shambled across the dining room, being the ape in Kuala Lumpur.

'Everywhere we went he followed,' Hilary said, waving her coffee spoon. 'We'd turn around quickly and he'd be peeping from behind a cage or a tree. And every time we looked he was just a little bit closer.'

Frank peeked around the door at us. A shy, sly ape.

'So we began hurrying,' he went on, and he pretended to be hurrying, 'until we'd gone all the way around the zoo and back to the turnstiles. The Sikh appeared, drinking a cup of tea, and said,' — and he did the funny voice again — '"From your heated condition, you have met our Mister Gibbon."'

We were all laughing when Frank sat down. Flushed and smiling, he topped up our port and cognac glasses. Eve caught my eye and smiled.

'And the gibbon?' Leo Cameron asked loudly. 'What about the gibbon?' Sometimes Leo's standing at the Bar inclines him to the brusque remark. 'I'd be asking why it was running around loose.'

Frank raised an eyebrow. 'The Indian said,' — and he did the voice again though with less enthusiasm — '"He will not bite you. Mister Gibbon is not a biter."'

'I suppose you heard,' said Leo, after a pause during which we laughed again, a little politely, and sipped fresh drinks, 'that Alan Dempster's boyfriend was bitten in half by a hippopotamus.'

He leaned back in his chair and waited until the

snorts and exclamations of disbelief had died down.

'You're kidding,' Frank said.

Leo cupped his brandy snifter in his palm. 'Alan and John went overseas each winter. They'd done Rio and the Caribbean and all the Pacific islands. This year they did Rhodesia.'

'I didn't know Alan Dempster was gay,' Hilary said.

'Oh, come *on*,' Sylvia Cameron said.

'No one tells me anything,' Hilary said. She drew on her cigarette and blew smoke over her shoulder.

'Let's hear about the hippo attack,' I said.

'The *alleged* hippo attack,' Frank said.

'Attack proven,' Leo said. 'They went on a scenic canoe ride on Lake Kariba. It must have been the mating season. This bull hippo charged the boat, up-ended it and snapped John in two.' He sipped his brandy thoughtfully. 'You've seen their jaws at the zoo, those whopping great teeth at feeding time? They can take a bucket of vegetables and two loaves of bread at a time. It doesn't touch the sides.'

'My God,' Eve said.

Sylvia said, 'Crocodiles I can understand. Lions and so on.'

'It's such an undignified way to go,' Eve said.

'It's more dignified to have your guts ripped out by a shark, is it?' Frank said. He preferred Margo, my first wife. 'To be bitten on the arse by a snake or something?'

'*I* think so,' Eve said.

'I fail to see the difference,' said Frank. He was looking intently at the brandy he was swirling around in his glass.

'I can see what Eve's getting at,' I said. I felt sorry for

96

her, tussling with Frank on his own territory, and I gave her knee a squeeze.

'A *dignified* death at all costs,' Frank murmured.

Leo spoke slowly and thoughtfully. 'The sad thing is that they salvaged only one half of John. It's buried up near his parents' place at Newcastle. Alan visits the grave quite regularly.'

'God!' Eve said.

'Which half?' Sylvia said. 'Don't tell me.'

'Wrong, darling,' Leo said, wagging a finger at her. 'The head and chest, actually.'

'Naughty, naughty,' Hilary said. 'I still can't get over Alan. He really likes women.'

Frank was tearing a wine cork to pieces. An earlier cork lay in a pyramid of crumbs on the tablecloth in front of him. 'A hippo attack?' he said. 'A man bitten in halves? Surely that would've made the front page of the *Mirror*. I didn't read a word.'

'I suggest you put your doubts to Alan Dempster,' Leo said. 'See what reaction you get.'

'Liking isn't doing,' Sylvia said.

'What I'm getting at,' said Eve, 'is that hippos look jolly and rubbery, like toys, not sort of sinister like sharks or snakes.'

'Absolutely,' I said. 'A friendly image.'

'Rubbery,' Frank said.

'No offence intended, but Alan made a fool of himself for years over that bitchy little cat,' Sylvia said.

'I find it very hard to imagine,' Hilary said.

Frank pushed himself up from the table and went for another bottle of port. When he returned he was smiling. 'At the other end of the animal scale,' he said, opening the bottle, 'and this definitely *did* make the

97

Mirror, did you read about the budgerigar at the talent quest?'

'Oh, not that,' Hilary said.

Frank was smiling wider as he re-filled the glasses. 'These two fellows had an act called The Death-Defying Budgie. They put this little blue budgie through various tricks, a tightrope walk and so on.' Frank made his fingers into a budgerigar and tiptoed them along the table. He made them hop and fly.

'I know what you're going to say, and I wish you wouldn't,' Hilary said, staring into her port.

'Try stopping Frank in full flight,' Leo said, giving his attention to a cigar. 'Frank the budgie.'

'This is the scene,' Frank said loudly. 'It's a boozy club out in the sticks, and they're the last act on. Tweety goes through his paces,' — Frank walked his fingers up the port bottle — 'except he muffs his last trick. It doesn't matter, the audience loves him. He's got the prize in the bag. They're all old girls, grandmas having a day out, got a budgie at home themselves. But one of Tweety's trainers is a perfectionist and he wants to put the bird through the routine again, get it right. The other guy disagrees, they have an argument on stage, and the perfectionist settles it by popping Tweety into his mouth and biting his head off.'

'Thanks, Frank,' Sylvia said. 'On top of Hilary's nice meal.'

'You won't be diverted, will you?' Hilary said.

'And swallows it!' Frank said. His cheekbones were flushed. 'You can imagine the disarray. Uproar. Fainting. Tears. There was a charge in it, too. The police were called. Aggravated cruelty to an animal. Our boy got a thousand dollar fine.'

'What about the contest?' I said. 'Did they win?'

Only Frank laughed. Eve widened her eyes at me and got up to go to the lavatory. 'Are you OK?' I asked her, patting her bottom as she passed.

'Yes,' she said. 'Don't forget we've got a busy day tomorrow.'

It infuriated me when Eve did that. It was always Eve who wanted to leave first, who broke up the party. A sudden decision seemed to come over her: all right, the party is over *now*. I don't often drink brandy because it makes my heart pound in the middle of the night, but while she was gone Frank passed the bottle with a wink and I poured myself a big one.

Sylvia wagged a finger at me. I sipped my cognac, felt it slide over my teeth and tongue and make them numb. Sylvia hunched toward me and spoke in a stage-whisper. 'How's Margo getting on?'

It had been five years; I had no idea how Margo was getting on. 'Fine,' I said. Just then Eve came back to the table. Her hair was freshly brushed. Sylvia winked elaborately at me and put a finger to her lips.

'We're here for the duration, are we?' said Eve as she sat down. She sounded like a headmistress or a hospital matron. Or a trial judge. She perched on the edge of her chair and fiddled with her place-mat in a self-righteous way. When she assumed that crisp manner a great gulf opened between us, as if by comparison I was a Skid Row derelict or something. At least Margo never did that. Margo liked a party.

'Well, I'm enjoying my brandy and the company,' I said, accepting one of Leo's cigars. The cigar somehow strengthened my resolve.

'I've got the taste too,' Frank said cheerfully, pouring

more brandy. He waved the bottle inquiringly in front of Eve but she sat with her hand over her glass like someone's maiden aunt.

Hilary turned to me and looked in my eyes. 'Alan is one who has never given me any clues at all,' she said. 'In what? Five, six, eight years?'

'Seriously?' Sylvia said. She laughed. 'With that neat little fellator's moustache?'

'Is that what they call them?' Hilary said.

'That neat little *solicitor*'s moustache,' Leo said. He was struggling to keep a straight face. 'I couldn't have been more sorry to hear the news,' he went on. 'I've always had a soft spot for Africa. Especially Rhodesia.'

'Zimbabwe,' Frank said. 'I let it pass last time.'

'Not to me, it isn't,' Leo said.

'Not that I would judge anyone else's situation,' Hilary went on. 'Who am I to judge anyone else's situation?' She gave a snort.

'Is that when you were last there, Leo?' Frank asked. 'With Cecil Rhodes?'

'Just about,' Sylvia said.

'I'm going to have to steal a cigarette if we're staying,' Eve announced. Obviously she had changed her mind about another drink: she was holding a glass of port.

Frank slid his cigarette case across the table. Eve was about to light one but debonair Leo beat her to it with his old Ronson. Eve drew on the cigarette and said loudly, 'I remember a camel in flames.'

After a moment Leo said, 'I beg your pardon?' Everyone was looking at Eve. She had raised her chin in that self-conscious, defiant way she had when she retreated into herself, into her life before me. No-one said anything.

Eve sipped her port. 'When I was a child in Armadale a circus came to town,' she said. 'The animals were grazing in a field and one of the camels burst into flames.'

'Struck by lightning,' Frank said.

'Definitely not,' said Eve. 'It just started burning. I remember it standing there in flames. It began moaning and bellowing and straining on its rope, and by the time the circus hands ran up with buckets of water it had burned up, just like a haystack on legs.'

'Spontaneous camel combustion!' Leo laughed. 'I like it.'

'Obviously lightning,' I said.

'Not at all,' said Eve. 'It was a fine day. Spring.'

'Funny that you haven't mentioned this before,' I said.

She looked at me. 'I just remembered it.'

'The Mystery of the Burning Camel,' Frank said, drawing the words out. 'If you don't mind me asking, Eve, were you under any strain at the time? Exams or puberty or what-have-you?'

'No, I wasn't.'

'Getting back to Africa,' Leo said, smiling all around. 'When *was* my last stretch out in the bush?' The question seemed directed at the table in general.

'*Bush*? I'm surprised you didn't say *veldt*,' Frank said. 'I was in Harare in eighty-seven, wasn't it, dear? For that torts convention?'

'I can't possibly remember them all,' Hilary said.

'Great for the tax,' Sylvia said, blowing smoke.

'The towns aren't Africa,' Leo said with relish, tilting back on his chair. 'The bush is the real Africa. The dusk, the sunsets, the dawns, the people, the animals, the blood.' The acoustics in the dining room seemed to have hardened. Leo's voice, the word *blood*, boomed off the walls. Years of advocacy reverberated over the table. 'The *basic* stuff. Origins. Survival. Richard Leakey. Back to Day One.'

Chad is Africa, I thought. I worry about Andrew in Africa. And Bolivia, the Middle East, the Golden Triangle. I lie awake anticipating a call from the embassy. The official notification. Some accident or other, some arrest or other, something awry in his luggage. I'm not convinced by 'native artifacts'. Where's the demand for ebony giraffes?

'Chad is Africa,' I said. Margo and I always wanted to go to Africa one day but the marriage ended before we made it. I was wondering if I could be bothered going there with Eve.

One moment Eve was sipping her port and the next I heard her voice in the corridor phoning a taxi. Sylvia was huddled with Hilary at the end of the table. Sylvia chuckled, stubbed out her cigarette, and she and Hilary joined Eve. For a while I heard them murmuring.

'Do you know what Africa is?' Leo asked suddenly, turning to me and raising his voice so that Sylvia and Hilary poked their heads back into the room. Leo's question hung in the air, crackling with static. 'Africa is danger,' he declared. 'And this isn't hearsay. This is *personal* experience, *life* experience, *Africa is a charging rhinoceros.*'

Frank put down his glass. 'Who hasn't been charged by a rhinoceros?'

Leo smiled like a lawyer and drew on his cigar. 'A *black* rhinoceros?'

Who can tell when something is about to go up in flames? How do you predict it? How should you react when it happens? As Eve's taxi pulled up and sounded its horn I took a big mouthful of brandy. I didn't get up.

THE NEEDLE 'STORY'

CHRISTINA LEE is taking her children to Canada to visit her brother and sister. 'I must have my family around me for a moment,' she says. The rest of her family immigrated recently to Toronto from Malaysia. Malaysia wasn't holding out as many prospects for non-Malays, for non-Muslims, for Chinese, as in the past. They felt the dice were loaded against them. Originally the family came from Shanghai, via Hong Kong. By 1950 they were all living in Malaya, as it was then, and Christina was born there.

So although the family has moved on (only an aunt and cousin of Walter's remain) there is still a deep attachment to Malaysia. That's why Christina is visiting Kuala Lumpur on her way to Toronto this summer: to take her husband's ashes back. She and the children, Adam, ten, and Felicity, eight, will spend three days in KL. There will be a small Baptist service there before they catch the Singapore Airlines flight to Vancouver.

SECRECY provisions prevent the Ombudsman from commenting specifically on any case. But I can say on

the record that if I find an unjust or defective adminis-
tration has disadvantaged someone I can make recommendations to the department concerned.

THE Malaysian-Chinese middle-class customarily
sends its children to universities abroad. Christina met
Walter at the University of Hong Kong. She was
studying arts, majoring in English literature. She was
intrigued by food in the writings of Charles Dickens:
Mr Micawber's Devilled Mutton, Mrs Wallmer's
Bread-and-Butter Pudding, and so on. Walter was
studying medicine. He was six years older and their
paths had scarcely crossed at home. He hadn't read
much Dickens, and certainly no puddings came to
mind. He seemed to recall a distinct lack of food in
Dickens — indeed, people asking for more. After their
marriage he practised both Western and traditional
Chinese medicine for several years in Malaysia before
they decided there were better opportunities for their
young children in Australia.

WESTERN Australia has the highest proportion of
Asian immigrants in Australia. This isn't surprising —
it's the nearest Australian State to Asia. It's also the
nearest Australian State to Africa, and has the highest
proportion of white emigrants from South Africa and
Zimbabwe, formerly Rhodesia. It is easy to see why
Western Australia is an attractive proposition for a
middle-class immigrant. Its climate ranges from sub-
tropical in the north to 'Mediterranean' in the more

populous south-west. Its economy is burgeoning. Its people are politically conservative but fiscally adventurous. Speculators are heroes here. 'Entrepreneur' is a flattering term. In many ways it is a pioneer society. There is good money to be made in real estate and mining speculation, and in the professions, too.

'I WOULDN'T want West Australians to feel I am fed up with Western Australia,' Christina Lee says defensively to a prickly blonde television reporter on her doorstep. People can take these things personally in isolated communities. No, she hasn't made up her mind whether to return. The reporter herself seems to be taking umbrage at the family's leaving, but maybe it's just the early hour of the news assignment, having to work on a Saturday, a hangover. There is still a sheen on the sea. The horizon is lost in mist. The camera shows Adam and Felicity dressed for the journey in the pale blue and gray summer uniforms of their private schools, Hale and St. Hilda's. Both schools are connected to the Anglican Church. Christina wears sun glasses and a floral dress in a subdued green and blue combination. She leaves the house at City Beach, the second City Beach house, with the blinds and shutters drawn against the anticipated summer heat, against the glare off the Indian Ocean and the white sand dunes. While she decides her future, a security service has been employed to guard against thieves, vandals and painters of graffiti. Is that one of its operatives already on the job, standing at ease in the corner of the screen, chewing gum and pulling his stomach in?

The ashes travel in a pewter flask in Christina's cabin luggage.

IT'S hardly necessary for the TV reporter to ask why she is leaving. Everyone here is familiar with the story. In fact, most people, including the Press, no longer see it as a 'story'. There is no 'story', they insist. Over and above the obvious one. A charlatan ripping off the system. A repeated offender. The TV reporter's touchy attitude implies not only that there is no 'story' any more, but that Christina has no right to try to make it one by appearing on her own doorstep on her way to the airport. Especially in the guise of a dignified widow with a small apologetic smile. That picture belongs to a different 'story' altogether.

Perhaps Christina could win over the TV reporter by weeping and producing the pewter flask for the camera. But it remains in her bag.

WHY is she leaving? For the same reason that she came. Because events led in that direction. Because events were set in train. But on-camera her answer is represented only by a small tight smile and a chin uplifted to the blurred north-west horizon.

EVENTS were set in train when Doctor Walter Lee set up his medical practice in West Perth, in a street lined with peppermint trees. Parliament House was a few blocks east; his neighbours were doctors, lawyers and mining companies. His practice prospered. Soon Walter and Christina each drove a Mercedes. They bought a big white house at City Beach, a prosperous suburb arranged on parallel hills of fine white sand facing the ocean. The sitting room and marital bedroom faced north-west towards Asia. The sun sank behind the high white limestone wall which sheltered the swimming pool from the afternoon sea breeze.

Even the swimming pool is part of the chain of events, part of the climate of fulfilled expectations which led to further expectations. In the pool Adam and Felicity were coached in their new swimming strokes. They were also coached in mathematics, science, tennis and music. On his one free evening a week Adam was a cub scout. His troop was chosen as part of the guard-of-honour at the garden party to enable the new State Governor, a retired and knighted English admiral, to meet the citizens of Western Australia — or those citizens fortunate enough to receive invitations. Adam learned that it was necessary for there to be twenty boy scouts on one side and twenty girl guides on the other side of the Government House steps — one boy and girl perched sideways facing each other on each narrow limestone step — so the Governor and his lady — in scout and guide uniforms — and their aides, could materialise at the top of the steps and walk slowly down through the lines of precariously balanced children to the citizens waiting below.

His father's was not among these eager upturned faces, but he was nonetheless proud of him. Walter was also proud of Adam's growing proficiency at the violin. He allowed only classical music to be played in the house, and in the waiting room of his medical practice. Mozart concertos mostly. Walter believed

111

they calmed his patients and helped the healing process. He prided himself on fostering a good doctor-patient relationship, and on helping his patients with a combination of Western medicine, acupuncture and massage. He was a local pioneer in the use of acupuncture. Most of his chronically ill patients came to him as a last resort and from all over the State.

CHRISTINA'S submission to the Ombudsman is couched in terms unlike her everyday speech. Her spoken English, although good, often slips inaccurately into the present tense. This can be disconcerting when she is discussing her husband. When questioned by the brusque young TV woman she finds it necessary to fix her gaze on the hazy horizon. She seems to be staring at an imaginary point about thirty kilometres north of Rottnest Island. The ocean is as calm as a swimming pool this early in the morning. Fishermen are still out: amateurs in dinghies powered by outboards. The tailor and whiting are running. Her face is composed behind her glasses. The plane leaves in two hours. 'Walter puts all his concentration into thinking about his patients,' she says to the horizon. 'Into doing what is best for them.' There is the small apologetic smile. 'A wonderful doctor, but clerically not so efficient. He leaves some things drift and antagonises the bureaucracy. We must go now.'

HER submission says: 'The circumstances and the lack of concern shown to my husband in the investigations which resulted in his being arrested and charged do not appear to be just.' She declares that this is her opinion and that of his colleagues, friends, patients and those members of the public 'familiar with the facts'. She feels it incumbent on her, for the sake of the children and her husband's good name, to vindicate him.

WALTER'S consulting rooms were near several voguish restaurants. It was fashionable for these restaurants to call themselves 'cafés' although they were by no means inexpensive and served elaborately designed food in which the element of difficulty often took precedence over subtlety of flavor in the chefs' priorities. These establishments were famous for their gastronomic ironies. Their reputations depended on their chefs producing tiny complex meals, but their chief customers, those who could afford their high prices, were self-made multi-millionaires, local heroes, whose appetites actually favored plainer, tastier food and bigger portions. The millionaires liked to be seen in these fashionable places, however, so they tipped hugely for their more basic tastes to be indulged. And the 'cafés' became cafés, dependent on the subsidised sale of grilled steak and fish.

Often, especially on Fridays, the doctor's driveway would be blocked between one and four pm by the millionaires' cars. He didn't make a fuss; he phoned the restaurants, gave the registration numbers and waited for an employee to come and shift the offending vehicles. Walter didn't frequent these fashionable places himself but bought Chinese or Malaysian take-away food from a café he knew which resisted the use of monosodium glutamate.

At home, for the evening meal with the children, Christina served 'English' food. Once or twice she drew on an amusing cookbook, *Mr Pickwick's Plentiful Portions*, which Walter had given her one Christmas and which brought back happy university memories.

Walter's friend Henry Lo, proprietor of the Golden Sun Café, took pride in not using monosodium glutamate in his cooking. Occasionally a new or lazy chef would try to sneak a jar of MSG into the café to flavor his recipes and Henry would throw it out. The doctor could always pick it. When he came to Australia he found that MSG was customarily added to all 'Asian' food. The Golden Sun was the first restaurant he had found to resist it. MSG gave him headaches, changed his moods and made him argumentative. He advised his patients to avoid it, especially those with hypertension or depression.

IN the first television film showing him arriving at court, Walter's eyes were dark and sunken. He looked mistrustfully at the cameraman. His haircut was fresh and raw; his straight hair stuck up at the sides like Dagwood's. He held a bag of his medical records in each hand. Preceding him up the courthouse steps, a bulky Federal policeman in a safari suit carried a carton of files.

Christina was in court. And his friend Henry Lo. The court was told that in Australia acupuncture was not recognised by the government, the health bureaucracy or the medical establishment as a 'treatment'. It was an 'attendance procedure'. Doctor Walter Lee had claimed it was a 'treatment'. He was consequently convicted of ten charges of pretending to give professional services. His actions had defrauded the government of a total sum of $173.80, the amount it had paid out to his patients in undeserved medical rebates. The judge gave him three years' jail.

CHRISTINA sold the two Mercedes, borrowed money from her family and assumed the dignified but apologetic smile at school functions. The children sometimes came home from school crying. Walter was folding towels in the prison laundry when he heard he'd been struck off the medical register; he didn't cry until he was back in his cell. The next day he began looking to religion for consolation. He started a Bible study class and led the prison prayer group.

When he was paroled for good behaviour in nine months, he sold the house built on white sand and took the family east to Sydney. He felt they had to leave Perth, but after the headlines his case had caused in Kuala Lumpur he couldn't face Malaysia. He seemed overcome by negativity and passivity. He began to get on Christina's nerves, hanging around their rented house in Willoughby all day, reading the Bible. He complained about the aggressive traffic and the rudeness of shop assistants. He was even querulous about the humidity, which was far lower than in Malaysia. He'd got used to the dry heat of Western Australia, the desert easterly and the regular sea breeze you could set your watch by. In Christina's opinion he was spending

115

too much time praying, attending a Baptist chapel in Chatswood every Sunday, even sharing communion mid-week in the living room of the local pastor. Christina wasn't enthusiastic about the Baptists. She said to pull up his socks and think of the children.

While he was praying for guidance she was contacting all his old colleagues and lobbying politicians. She was also working on him, reminding him of Western Australia's attractions. The dry heat. The quiet traffic. She brought up Hale and St. Hilda's, swimming, tennis, the violin and boy scout guards-of-honour. She was hopeful that the past had been forgiven and that his patients would return to him.

The second City Beach house was smaller, but with a similar ocean view. In place of the Mercedes they each drove a Toyota. After six months Christina's campaign for Walter's readmittance by the Medical Board was successful. He began practising medicine again just a block from his old rooms. Henry Lo threw a welcome-back party at the Golden Sun. It was mostly Cantonese food, using local ingredients: abalone and spinach soup, pork spare-ribs with cumquat sauce, asparagus chicken, prawns and braised almonds, blue manna crabs in black bean sauce, dhufish in special sauce. With the meal Henry served local Chablis, Chardonnay and beer. 'For this banquet you can fix my uric acid,' Henry joked to Walter, flexing his knuckles with a grimace. 'Ease up on the protein,' Walter said. 'You're an Asian, remember.'

LOOK, I can only say that my recommendations are pretty specific in character. Offhand, I'd say that a substantial inquiry involving people in two or three States would take several months. Of course, a department is not bound to follow my recommendations, but I am empowered to take the matter all the way to the Prime Minister and ask that he take action.

THERE is minor disagreement on the numbers of Federal police who took part in the second raid. Christina remembers six, the receptionist, Geraldine McCuskey, eight. They agree that two of the police entered the surgery smoking cigarettes and that one of them flicked his ash on the floor and rubbed it in with his shoe. They agree there was no search warrant. The police told the patients to go home. They took away all Walter's files and patients' records, his account and receipt books and any reference to the word 'acupuncture'. They confiscated twelve acupuncture needles and two syringes. And they arrested him.

CHRISTINA could have told the prickly TV reporter of several aspects of life in Western Australia she found bemusing. For example, she was vaguely curious about the relationship between elderly vice-royalty and young boy scouts and girl guides. She wondered why jewfish was spelled *dhufish*, why so many voices on talk-back radio had north of England or South African accents, why it took so many police to arrest a short, harmless doctor, why he had been locked up and why the bail was set at sixty thousand dollars.

*   *   *

117

CHRISTINA appeared at the lock-up with real estate sureties for the second house at City Beach. They kept Walter inside for four hours, then released him on bail. He was ordered to appear in court in eight days' time on three counts of making false statements regarding medical treatments. The amount of money involved came to fifty-one dollars.

AROUND the courthouse, in the north of the city, the streets are noticeably 'foreign' and raffish. In the old days there was a street of brothels here to service lonely migrants and the American fleet on its regular visits. Now there are nightclubs and bars and restaurants serving food of many nations. One of the Chinese restaurants, the Jade Palace, is popular with the lawyers, detectives and magistrates attending the court. Walter's solicitor, Michael Thody, is a regular customer, a member of a lunch group which eats there every Friday. The other members are a stockbroker, two sportswriters, a real estate agent, a retired footballer turned TV weatherman, a horse trainer and a dentist. It's an informal and rowdy group; the members don't stand on ceremony, and they often bring other guests. A feature of the Friday lunches is the jocular abuse the members heap on the proprietor, amiable Richard Luey, and his wife Rose.

WHEN Walter next appeared in court it was a Friday morning. Thody represented him. The hearing was very short. Although Walter stood in the dock he was not required to plead and was remanded to appear

118

again in another eight days while the prosecution organised its case. The magistrate agreed to the prosecution's request that Walter surrender his passport and report to the police twice a week.

Walter stepped down from the dock and left the courtroom. Thody followed him. In the corridor Thody lit a cigarette and stuffed briefs into his briefcase. Luckless shabby people shuffled past. A whiff of phenol came from somewhere. Walter collapsed onto a bench and painstakingly blew his nose into a blue handkerchief. Thody looked at his watch and then at his desolate client, still working on his nose. It was 12.23. 'Join me for lunch,' Thody invited him. 'Chinese,' he added.

An hour later Thody was asking himself why he'd made the invitation. Because he had a son at Hale, too. And the doctor was having a rough time. But it was a mistake; his presence was a great damper. It had an inhibiting effect on the jokes and gossip and made their usual banter with Richard and Rose Luey seem crude and embarrassing. The doctor's heart wasn't in it, anyway. He didn't touch the wine. He just put his head down and shovelled the food in, chopsticks flashing. Apart from the Jade Palace staff he was the only Chinese in the room. Thody wondered whether it was the first time he'd ever been to an Australian social gathering.

WHEN Christina came home from the New World supermarket with the weekend groceries he was sitting in his armchair reading the Bible aloud. The sight of him abject and muttering shocked her. She put down the supermarket bags and went to him. How are you? Where have you been? What happens now? She remembers asking such questions, showing concern. Concern, but not love. It was hard to show love, to console him, while he was chanting from the Gospels with red-rimmed Baptist eyes, and soy sauce on his tie. 'You look at me strangely,' he suddenly accused her. 'As if I were a criminal.' Tears shot from his eyes. He jumped up and the Bible fell to the floor. 'You are a stranger to me,' he shouted. 'You always have been. I am alone, completely alone.' He cursed her and stormed around the house, his eyes puffy, a handkerchief to his nose. Christina left the groceries on the kitchen floor and ran out to her car. She had to collect the children. From school, from swimming, tennis, music, scouts. She had to leave the house and Walter's angry presence. In thirteen years he had never raised his voice at her.

Walter took some aspirin for his headache. Then he picked up his medical bag, got into his car and drove into the city. He checked into the top hotel, into a room facing north-west. He injected himself with an overdose of morphine and pethidine and lay back on the bed.

THIS case could go on for a long time. I can say no more than that. Even before we decide whether to proceed there are several departments to consider, rosters, holidays, et cetera, to take into account. There is a mass of material to study: legal documents, court records, technical and medical data, statements from individuals. And there is the question of Common-

120

wealth/State liaison, always a ticklish one. I would say you're looking at nine or ten months at the earliest. More likely twelve. And I hear the widow is leaving the country. That won't make things easier. This is totally off the record, of course.

CHRISTINA ushers the children through the metal detector into the departure lounge. She has been worrying for days that the pewter flask will cause trouble. She has envisaged alarms, disruption, questions, embarrassing explanations. Inside her bag, however, presently moving along the conveyor into the X-ray machine, and of unthreatening shape, it passes through without a hitch.

ALL THE BOYS

WHEN last seen by David and Angela Lang, the Cabinet Minister was reading the palm of a call-girl in the Top of the Mark, the roof lounge of the Mark Hopkins Hotel in San Francisco.

The call-girl's palm was his third in five minutes. Six people were having after-dinner drinks. The call-girl was the only American in the group. It was a clear evening in August 1980 and the green and pastel hills of the city rose and fell around them. The Presidential election was in the air.

OVER the racket the lawn-mower woman complains that doctors won't do circumcisions these days. Pregnancy has made her even more talkative, if anything. Nothing shows yet under the heavy sweater. Her pink cheeks are speckled with chopped grass ends. Fair hair trails out of her woollen cap. She really has to put her shoulders behind the mower in that thick marshy patch near the drain.

Lang is a little startled at her boldness, at the way this image sticks to her right away. Maybe if he was still her age, the casual early-twenties, and an acceptable challenge, he'd be able to confront her and her

125

metaphors. ('You're really into cutting, eh?') If he wasn't more or less her employer. If her appeal wasn't so instinctual. If she wasn't the lawn-mower woman, and pregnant.

'You try to get a doctor to do one!' she shouts at him. 'Just try!'

THE Minister was noisy and hearty. He showed surprise at the degree of passion implied in the call-girl's love line. But he had already chuckled with astonishment at each of the other two women's love lines, so he went further. His index finger traced the line on the call-girl's palm, tickled it, and then he said, 'My goodness!', his eyes twinkling and a gold filling gleaming in his smile. At the same time he raised those avuncular eyebrows which were such a boon to the cartoonists.

'What have we here?' he said.

THE lawn-mower woman's name is Astrid. Her accent still has some guttural traces. Her husband — presently pushing the second mower up the slope behind the house — is Dennis. Astrid talks, shouts, about him all the time. Pushing through the juicy buffalo, she tells Lang, 'I made Dennis have a naughty every night for three months until one took.' She is rosy and pretty, very white-toothed when she laughs. 'Dennis said, "Can I have a rest now?"'

POLITICS: before the Minister's arrival the talk at the Top of the Mark was about the election. The Democratic convention had just ended in anti-climax. The American Embassy hostages were still in Iran. When their attempted rescue failed dismally Jimmy Carter's stocks had plummeted even further. Nevertheless the careworn President had withstood a half-hearted challenge from Teddy Kennedy. In the Republican primaries Ronald Reagan was drawing away from George Bush and Howard Baker and could conceivably — to the foreigners, amazingly '— win the nomination.

Lang agreed with Peter Boyle that Carter was a goner. He recalled the mood down on California and Filmore streets, at the Minit-Market, the Texaco station, even the frozen yoghurt bar (where, in the peace murals and Dylan tapes, the last decade's political fashions clung tenaciously), when news of the abortive rescue got out. People took it personally, especially the men. The grey-faced old checkout clerk at the Minit-Market shook his head all day. His fingers stabbed at the cash-register keys. 'Goddamn, I think of Ike,' he said. 'Truman. Ford, even!'

Boyle announced loudly that Americans' virility was bound up in them winning these tussles. 'The government botches a gung-ho operation like this and guys all over the country can't get it up that night.'

Coming from a country with lower expectations, the Australians around the table all laughed. Lang said, 'Speaking of which, did you read the Updike story in the *New Yorker*, about this fellow whose wife suddenly couldn't climax? There was this heavy snowstorm and their car was snowed in. He shovelled away manfully, all the time giving precise instructions to his wife behind the wheel ...'

'Wife behind the wheel?' Boyle cut in. 'Sounds right.'

'They got the car out,' Lang went on, 'and she was full of compliments for him, for his physicality and

127

intelligence, and *Shazam*, their sex life took off again.'

'Naturally,' Angela said.

'Excuse me,' said the call-girl, 'but aren't we forgetting the hostages here? The human element. That saddens all of us, the idea of Americans suffering.'

THUS while he sits on the front step with his breakfast mug of tea, Lang learns that cutting lawns ten hours a day takes it out of Dennis. But they can't complain, Astrid says. (He has brought her a cup of tea too, which she downs in three swigs.) Things are going according to plan. When he was a clerk in the Lands Department Dennis had studied all the rainfall maps and discovered that the conjunction of the ranges and the coastline and the southerlies made Charlotte Bay the wettest town in the State. All that rain must mean quick-growing grass, Dennis reasoned, correctly. You couldn't let your lawn go more than a fortnight. Better still, half these places were weekenders, holiday cottages, whose owners didn't want to come down that often just to cut grass.

'So we came down here and gave it the once-over,' Astrid says. *Wunz-offer*. 'Fan-tastic!'

David Lang used to be one of those intermittent weekend visitors. Now he has moved down here and runs his architectural office from what was the cottage's main bedroom. He has made changes right across the board, but he hasn't thought of changing the lawn mowing arrangements. His lawn mowing contractors have not shown the slightest curiosity at his being in residence every day. He isn't sure whether he wants Astrid to be curious or not.

*   *   *

THE Langs were spending a sabbatical year at Stanford and Berkeley, renting an apartment between the two campuses in lower Pacific Heights. Peter and Fiona Boyle were up from their home in Malibu and had suggested dinner. Boyle was a wealthy expatriate from Sydney. During the meal he had mentioned running into the Minister in Union Square that afternoon. He'd suggested he join them later for a drink.

Although politics was in the air, it wasn't politics which had brought the Minister to America. 'He's here as patron of some sporting foundation,' Boyle said. 'Wheelchair athletes, caber-tossers, some junket like that.' He snorted with amusement. 'I was walking past the consulate and this black limo was at the curb with its little Australian flag flying. He steps out, spots me and calls out in the middle of Post Street, "Hey, Peter! Where can I get a girl?"'

ASTRID is looping her way around the tree stump, ducking under the weeping-willow fronds and heading back to him. Her mowed trail, a deeper green, makes the shape of a dented egg, a child's puzzle, a target. The morning sun is still low; the unmown grass is silver-tipped. Dew sprays away from Astrid's gumboots as she comes nearer, shouting again.

'"Give me a reason," they all say. "Because it's cleaner," I say, "safer from disease." They give me funny looks. "Nonsense," they say. "Give me another." "Religion then." They don't go for that either. Very sarcastic. "Is that so, Mrs McGuinness? Jewish, are you? It's mutilation these days," they say. "An obscure religious rite. In good conscience we can't cut."' She shakes her head as she passes, but she's still smiling.

The grass is so spongy that her trail is imprinted with her boot heels. She can't be more than four months pregnant and it mightn't even be a boy!

DISCUSSING the events of the evening later, the Langs differed only on the color of the call-girl's hair. He said auburn, she said brown. They agreed she was quite attractive, not flamboyantly so, not exactly *sexy*, but tastefully dressed and an intelligent and polite conversationalist. (She said she had studied political science and literature at Berkeley.)

(Actually, he found the call-girl intriguing and most attractive. She had pearly skin and a serious frown. Before the Minister arrived they had talked of literature, too. The call-girl was romantically inclined towards Camus and Tolstoy, perhaps because of their errant youth.

'Tolstoy was really *mad*,' she said. 'I mean totally *insane*.' The corners of her mouth turned up in pleasure. Her grey eyes shone. 'At the siege of Sebastopol, Tolstoy jumped out of the trenches and ran towards the bastion under heavy fire from the enemy. He was *really* afraid of rats, and he'd just seen one and freaked out.')

David and Angela also agreed on the timing of the after-dinner arrivals. The call-girl, Kathy, had arrived at the Top of the Mark forty minutes before the Minister. By the time he turned up, a frisson of amused anticipation was building up.

Certainly the Langs had nudged each other at his entrance, at his edgy adjustment of his tie in the doorway, the practised keen frown, the sudden little spring of feigned youth in his step — and the momentary flicker of confusion when faced with three young-ish attractive women.

Although only one of the women had an American accent, and Boyle introduced them all, the Minister seemed unsure which was his escort. Had he forgotten, or not known, her name? Or was it just that he couldn't resist working the room?

Perhaps he was acting decisively after all, boldly facing his dilemma, by striding over to the table, greeting Boyle, then squeezing himself between the nearest women, Fiona and Angela, and immediately swinging into a routine of masculine chuckles and rakish ploys. In no time he was reading Fiona's palm, then Angela's, and uncovering voluptuous secrets. Then he guessed at sensual star signs. He dominated the conversation. He showered the table with debonair innuendo from the Age of Aquarius (when he would have been in his forties), and his hands brushed knees and patted shoulders with dog-paw familiarity.

The Minister was a spruce and eager spaniel. Boyle watched his performance with quiet satisfaction, allowing some time to pass before announcing solemnly, 'Minister, may I present, at the far end of the table, Ms Kathy Molera, your companion for this evening.' Shameless, the Minister pushed back his chair, bounded to her side and snatched up her hand.

The Langs wondered why he felt bound to flirt with her, to win her over.

ASTRID is smiling at *herself*, Lang realises as she rounds the tree stump again, panting slightly, as much from excitement as the exercise. She loves her condition and is in awe of it. Her sweater has snowmen across the breasts. Her skin is delicate and proud. 'All the boys in Den's family are circumcised!' she calls out. 'All Irish Catholic boys!'

She whirs past him with an inquiring grin.

BACK home in Sydney, the Langs would exchange knowing smiles whenever the Minster's name came up, especially in dinner party conversation with people who, unlike them, voted for his party. One of them would say, 'Have we ever told you about our evening with him and the call-girl in San Francisco?'

It made a good story. They enjoyed relating how a Californian call-girl had instructed a leading politician on American politics. In the call-girl's overview of the election she had mentioned the name 'Tip O'Neill' and the Minister had asked loudly, 'Who's Tip O'Neill?'

'The Speaker,' she said. 'The presiding officer in the House of Representatives. The Number Three Man. If an assassin shoots the President *and* the Vice-President, he's *it*. He takes over.'

The Minister sat up straight and his chin firmed. 'Of course,' he said.

In the next eight years — during which time the Minister's party lost office and he retired from politics, and the Langs' marriage broke up — if they thought of him at all it was less as a politician and public figure than as the doggy philanderer at the Mark Hopkins. The politician who read women's palms and hadn't heard of Tip O'Neill.

THE coastline at Charlotte Bay is always moist and green and gives the impression of trying to imitate Ireland. A choppy surf throws kelp on to the wide

132

white beach. The legs of the local children are stained with clay. People tug woollen caps in the colors of football teams over their ears. Mists edge around the hill tops and sea fogs hang over the crayboat harbour. Much of the grazing land is overrun with blackberries. The general store displays gumboots and balaclavas alongside the scuba equipment and blackberry poison right through summer. The townspeople discourage conversation or commerce with newcomers or visitors, opening their shops late and closing early and randomly throughout the day.

But Lang's business, designing timber coastal retreats for city people, is just healthy enough. So is he. He swims on sunny days the year round, trekking across the pale dunes to the cold but restorative sea. His only competition is nature: the artfully placed and engineered spider web under the veranda light; the perfect pink circles of jellyfish on the beach (the jellied coronas melting into the sand) arouse his professional awe. The tension and thrust in a eucalypt twig rebounding from an abruptly departing parrakeet — this can stop him in his tracks. And the shocking void of the parrakeet's absence. Above his veranda the purple and green sky skews towards vivid bruised sunsets, and competing rainbows arch the horizon and hills. In such circumstances the beauty of the bay can bring on melancholy and loneliness.

ALTHOUGH the ground is damp, the day is dry and sunny on the mid-winter's morning that the papers announce the former Minister's death. The lawn mowers clatter in the yard. Lang opens the paper and reads the news sitting in the patch of sunlight spreading across his front step. It is cautiously presented in a single-column story adjoining a sedate obituary which outlines his 'industrious and quietly effective' political career.

His body was found in a motel in the Sydney suburbs. At his age, sixty-three, a heart attack was presumed. According to the police there were no suspicious circumstances. The former Minister had checked into the motel alone on Saturday and dined that evening with friends. A housemaid discovered his body in bed at noon on Sunday. An autopsy would be held. A final paragraph, an apologetic-sounding addendum, noted that the police would like to interview a woman seen in his company in the motel lobby late on Saturday night.

LANG makes a point of being at his drawing-board before nine. Working from home, it would be easy to slip into lazy habits. But this morning before he starts work he phones Angela, from whom he has been divorced for four years. Astrid and her racket loop around the tree and head back. He closes the window against the noise. 'It's me,' he says. 'Did you see the paper?'

'Oh, I was just about to call you.' Her voice is high and lively, with its old optimistic inflections. 'Well, well,' she says. 'We could have predicted it, couldn't we?'

'Absolutely, if anyone could. Silly old bastard.'

'I'll never forget the look on his face when Peter pointed out which girl was the prostitute.'

Lang mimics the Minister's hollow, booming voice: 'Who's Tip O'Neill?' Then he goes on, 'Look at that love line! Darling, I'd be careful of that warm heart of yours.'

'Yes, yes,' she laughs. 'Exactly right!' He can imagine her clapping her hands. The young wife delighted with his cleverness. 'What a night!' she says.

'Extraordinary.'

'Well, he probably died happy. But I bet this one wasn't as classy as that girl in San Francisco.'

'Not likely.'

Her voice is still animated. 'It's funny how often I think of that year.'

'Yep.'

'Oh, Dave, didn't we do some things then?'

'That's right.' Even as he agrees with her he is actually remembering her ten years before then, in her twenties. When he feels sentimental and nostalgic, she is always in her twenties — eager and idealistic, wafting around with long hair, in loose dresses. Young women wafted back then; in his best years young women wafted and tinkled and gave off spicy scents. Pieces of mirror shone in their dresses.

'Well, I mustn't keep you,' she says.

THE afternoon paper isn't as reticent as the morning papers. It likes the idea of the 'mystery woman' who was 'entertained' by the ex-Minister. Its emphasis evokes a *femme fatale*, a Mata Hari figure. The paper says she is still being sought by the police for questioning. Evidence showed, the paper says — without elaborating — that she was with him when he died.

The paper carries brief interviews with the night manager of the motel ('They both looked in good spirits when they went upstairs at 11.30'), the waitress who served him dinner ('He joked with me and seemed very charming; his party drank white and red wine, then had port and cigars') and two bluffly defensive political cronies who assert that their old colleague was 'as straight as a die', 'the most honest man in politics' and 'the ultimate party man'.

The Prime Minister is quoted as saying that while he and the former Minister hadn't always seen eye to eye on political matters he had always respected him personally for his integrity and energy.

Lang digests this news while he splits ironwood logs for firewood with a sledgehammer and wedge. He has started to do 'useful' exercise each evening, and he likes the idea of providing his own firewood. As each hammer blow rings through his skull, however, jars his arms and sends shock waves through his shoulders and into his lower back, it occurs to him that this 'exercise' weakens as it strengthens. Not only is it probably worse for him than it is beneficial, but he is paying people to mow his lawn, a job so easy that a pregnant woman can manage it. And a winter's firewood supply costs far less than a winter's lawn-mowing services. Is this a logical way to lead your life?

Before dinner, resting his back in front of the fire, he keenly watches the TV news, switching channels to follow the story. Each channel has sent a reporter to stand in front of the motel where the ex-Minister died, but the story is far from being the lead item. None takes it further than reporting that the postmortem examination confirmed a heart attack and that a state funeral will be held. The 'mystery woman' of the afternoon paper still showed no inclination to come forward.

Each reporter seems to be having trouble keeping a straight face.

By next morning the ex-Minister's career has been thoroughly reappraised. The serious political columnists argue that his influence on his party, much less on national politics, was negligible. Their main theme is that an early talent was frittered away in a vain and vacuous middle-age. One columnist goes so far as to say that the Minister's prominence in his party was instrumental in keeping it out of office.

The re-appraisal continues during the day. In the main street a poster outside the newsagent shrieks at Lang: *Night of Fatal Sex*. It is a notorious scandal sheet which finds its way even to Charlotte Bay, boasting of having 'the full story' on the death at the motel. Shamelessly, given the shopkeeper's wife's disapproving frown, Lang buys a copy. This tabloid mentions 'the well-kept secret in political circles of his penchant for nubile young women'. It also elaborates on the detail that even the afternoon paper had shied from (and that gave the TV reporters their smirks), the evidence that he wasn't alone when he died. The body, announces the scandal sheet, was still wearing a condom.

ANGELA calls *him* this time. Her voice is pitched lower today. 'Everything OK?' he asks. Her moods always used to be up and down. Just the fact of her making the phone call indicates something.

'Oh, I don't know. I just feel terrible about what they're doing to him. Our palm-reading friend.' And she hadn't even heard yet about the rigor mortis. After a pause she says, 'That's just too much. What do they think they're doing, these people? These little twirps?'

'Tough on the wife and family, you mean?'

'Yes, them too. It just seems like, well, nothing more than bad luck. It's not as if he was corrupt or anything. He wasn't *evil*.'

Lang is surprised at the change in her. She isn't giving the wife the moral weight she once would have. All the moral weight. She has changed her emphasis. 'No,' he says. 'Of course he wasn't evil. He just died on the job. Good luck to him.'

'It's not exactly unknown. The combination of age and excitement and stress and so on. New partners. There's a lot of it about.'

'Is that so?' He has kept her private life well out of his mind. She wears more make-up these days, dresses more blatantly. On her clothesline he's spotted black underwear of a mistressy wispiness.

'Don't tell me it hasn't occurred to you?' she says, and makes a sound like a laugh.

IT has occurred to him. His father died in a hotel room. On a tourist island, naked, but not — according to the hotel manager's evidence at the inquest — wearing a condom. Alone? Who knows? He was there on business, a convention. 'There was a towel draped over his loins,' the manager told the coroner. He had trouble with the word 'loins'. He was defensive. Deaths were bad for business. The manager had it in for his father for dying. He said, 'He was a man who'd been in the sun but his skin looked mottled to me.'

Lang came north for the inquest. He heard a doctor say there was a medical term for his father's final

138

behaviour: his getting out of bed, going to the bathroom, dying on the bathroom floor. Neatly, with the towel over his genitals: Anguish of the Soul. *Angor animi*.

'What happens,' the doctor told the court, 'is that when the heart attack is coming on they get a sense of impending doom. A-n-g-o-r a-n-i-m-i,' he spelt it out for the court typist. 'They experience this sense of doom, they defecate, then they die.'

But not before they'd tidied themselves up. 'What colour was the towel?' asked the coroner. 'Which way was it draped? Lengthways? Sideways across the body?'

The answer was white and sideways. Anguish of the Soul.

IT has occurred to him. Sometimes, in the split-second before the engulfment, the explosion of atoms, the thought is actually part of it: *This is it. I don't care if I die now*! But a little later he reneges and hopes otherwise, with all his heart.

HIS father was circumcised. Like father, like son in those days. But these tribal customs don't have to go on for ever. He broke the chain: Paul, his elder son, was, Tim, the younger, wasn't. Everyone represents an era of medical fashion. He doesn't have an ideological or religious position on this, but maybe an unnecessary operation on a newborn baby isn't a good idea. Surely Astrid would appreciate that. He should remind her that tonsillectomies were all the rage in his childhood — now whose kid ever has one?

Astrid is a throwback to the generation of the knife.

*   *   *

139

THE last time he saw his father he was eating mud crab at Doyle's with a bib around his neck. He was teasing waitresses. They sat under an umbrella with the April sun slanting across the table. His father flirted with waitresses with his second wife smiling at him and a bib around his neck and crabmeat on his cheeks and fingers. He was pink from the sun and Chablis. He splashed in his finger bowl like a big happy baby.

ASTRID has 'naughties'. He imagines a 'naughty' 'taking' inside Astrid.

HE can really draw the paper out these mornings. The editorials, letters, sport, finance, what used to be called the 'women's' pages. *You and Your Health* was canvassing the circumcision question. *You and Your Health* came out in favor. Current medical thinking, it said, was swinging back to circumcision. Removing the foreskin seemed to lessen urinary tract infections in young boys and might even lessen the chances of cervical cancer in the boys' future sexual partners.

Astrid was in the vanguard of medical knowledge! Astrid was on the wavelength of her generation!

THE papers also carry solemn photographs of the state funeral, lists of mourners and excerpts from the eulogies. Apparently an archbishop spoke approvingly and the Prime Minister sent his deputy. No critical note marred the occasion or mars its representation.

'DID you read about the funeral?' This time he has telephoned her. It's nine in the morning again and he's doodling on his drawing board, sketches of birds. Outside, two magpies peck at the lawn. Already the grass has grown a couple of inches. He can tell the sex of magpies these days: the female is grey-necked, the male's the one with the crisp white neck feathers. No warbling this morning, just a wary-eyed domestic couple breakfasting together.

'I saw it on TV. The typical roll-up, all the politicians looking very po-faced. What got me,' she suddenly says in her old animated voice, 'was how sanctimonious everyone became all of a sudden.'

'A case of "There but for the grace of God ..."'

'Exactly.'

'The wife took it very well,' he says.

'Mmm.' There is a pause, a tiny vacuum, as if she's shifting the phone to the other ear. 'I hear they'd been separated for years. And guess what? The mystery woman has come forward — three of them!'

'You're kidding!'

'Two socialites, via statements from their lawyers saying that vile rumours were spreading and it wasn't them, and an escort-agency girl saying she thinks it was her but she isn't sure.'

'She *thinks* it was her? How many customers does she lose a night?'

'Apparently escort girls depart very speedily.'

'Where did you hear all this?' He is impressed. 'I didn't read this anywhere.'

'Of course not. You're out of touch down there in Sleepy Hollow.'

'You better fill me in.' The companionable phone is on his ear. He and Angela gossip and banter. He looks out the window and doodles birds. He is feeling so

141

jovial he could invite her down there one weekend. She is chatting and chatting, in full stride, and he is doodling magpies and smiling into the phone at her breathless rush, leaning back in his chair and encompassing the mood, the morning. The lawn is lush and glistening with dew. Surely it's growing as he looks at it. Near the drain it's impossibly green and springing up fast from Astrid's heel marks.

'Did you see that circumcision is making a comeback?' he says.

'Did it ever die out?'

'Seriously, current medical opinion is for it again. What about poor old Timmy? Did we do the wrong thing? Or not do the right thing?'

Who is a greater male chauvinist than a doting mother of sons? She laughs a jovial, callous laugh. 'Tim is fine. He's a charmer. He'll do all right for himself.'

As this jolly, coarse stranger jokes on, the sun spreads over the lawn. The grass looks luxuriant enough to stroke or eat. You could roll in it, he thinks, graze on it. It could sustain life. He is unreasonably excited at the grass growing so quickly. From a nearby yard comes the buzz of mowers. He feels far too dazed and youthful to investigate metaphors. He scribbles the words *grass is grass* and thinks of women.

SISTER

WHEN our mother died suddenly no one told my sister for six days. 'I'll be the one to tell Annie,' Dad insisted. He was grey with shock. He asked her friend Deidre's mother, Mrs Duncan, to look after Annie until after the funeral. He said things would be calmer then.

Before their marriage my mother was a Catholic; the funeral service was Presbyterian. In Dad's circle of friends only men went to funerals. Protestant business acquaintances, yes; daughters, and sons under fourteen, no. At fourteen I just scraped in. Max, thirteen, didn't make it. Actually, he was relieved. 'It'd make me too unhappy,' he told me. I could see his point. But there was no sobbing or untoward emotion. Dad's eyes looked rheumy and at one stage at the graveside I wept, at the crucial moment, but Mr Johnstone of Johnstone Automotive Industries caught my eye and I stopped. The question of open coffins or saying goodbye or any of that business just didn't arise.

Dad's intention was to minimise the upset. He wanted to protect Annie's feelings. 'She's only eight,' he'd groan of an evening, every evening that first week. They went very slowly, especially with TV not allowed. He'd think out loud for five or six hours and drink a lot of Dimple Haig.

145

Eventually Dad had to collect Annie from Mrs Duncan's. Max and I were watching when they came home. Dad helped her out of the car like a little invalid, but she looked just the same, only quieter and more wary. At the Duncans there had been vague talk of illness, hospitals, even 'journeys'. Dad led her gently into the back garden. He'd given this six evenings' thought. He gave her a posy of flowers from the funeral service. He gave her Mum's wedding, engagement and eternity rings. Then, by the rose-beds, he gave her the news.

She frowned up from her palm full of rings and saw me watching. Her expression became strange — calm, wise, self-contained. She looked like a sorrowful adult to whom all things had suddenly become clear.

Six days before, two hours after the ambulance left, she had run in from school as usual, with her usual cry. 'Hey, Mummy,' she called. 'Is there a mother there?' She was surprised to see me home so early. I was sitting on the veranda, staring outwards. The sky was unfamiliar to me; the trees in the garden, the respective colors, even the angles and outline of our house looked different. People had careless faces.

I was an accomplice in this unreality. 'What mother?' I shouted, as some woman or other rushed out and hurried Annie over to Mrs Duncan's.

LIFE OF A BARBARIAN

WHEN the earthquake strikes, Michael Pond is trying to wash away his hangover in the shower. Suddenly the floor of the shower cabinet slides from under his feet. As he slips, he twists his back and bumps his head on the wall. Landing heavily on his buttocks, he sits staring stupidly at his courtesy toiletries hopping along the edge of the washbasin and dropping to the floor.

Six point five on the Richter scale; the whole hotel is waving like a blade of grass. Luckily the epicentre is well north of Tokyo. For a second the earth seems to be opening beneath Pond, and his runaway razor and toothpaste and miniature soaps and smashed bottle of *Eau Sauvage* are portents of the end.

But as time expands and the bathroom keeps undulating he becomes fatalistic. He feels silly, nearly amused, as if he's in an animated cartoon. He can see himself sitting on the floor watching the waving walls with his mouth in a surprised O. He wipes up the broken glass with a towel, and then the past twenty-four hours get too much for him. Still half-wet, he climbs back into bed and collapses.

*   *   *

A LONG flight from Australia, with the usual drinks on the plane and more when they reach the Imperial and check in. Then when Dick Hannam from Trade suggests going out on the town a few of the delegation urge each other along. Pond succumbs.

At one-thirty they end up in this place Dick knows. The mama-san is just closing for the night but she asks them to wait while she organises the girls.

The waiting room takes some of the wind out of their sails. Suddenly it's something like the dentist's, with the seascape prints and stacks of magazines and a big tank of tropical fish in the reception area. But a dentist of dreams. There is a TV set in a corner and an old man is glued to it, watching a game show. Three stony-faced Japanese men, presumably the winning contestants, file past four bare-breasted hostesses. The game-show host, dropping his clipboard to demonstrate, urges the men to tweak the women's nipples. This seems to be their prize.

Pond can't believe what he's seeing. 'Hey!' he says to the others. The prizewinners meanwhile give about five seconds' attention to each nipple, shuffling sideways between the hostesses. While the men are as serious as safe-crackers seeking the right combination, the women look over the prizewinners' earnest heads and twitter at the camera, showing green teeth. The program's color is richly askew. The teeth and flesh of the beaming hostesses, the men's square faces, are different shades of green; the women's lips are black and everyone is dressed in purple.

THE woman who leads Pond away is sullen at having to work late. She makes his bath water too hot on purpose and orders him into it with bossy gestures. Like a lobster steaming on a rack, he sits panting on the wooden bath mat while she flicks around the room gathering towels and adjusting water pressures.

When she comes in her white tunic to wash him she is as brisk and efficient as a nurse, not an image or procedure which overly excites him. The room fittings smell of rubber. An antiseptic steam rises from the bath. The sterile surroundings, somewhere between a laboratory and an operating theatre, make Pond feel helpless and alien, like an ape awaiting vivisection.

When she orders him from the bath he stands up and doesn't recognise his flesh. He is astonishingly red and hairy, more gross than he's ever noticed. He sags from the heat. Towering over the grumpy girl, sweat dripping from his chin, he mimes urgent drinking motions. 'Cold water,' he says.

Crossly, she unfurls a hose and mutters something. He drinks from it and runs water over his head. She regains the advantage by towelling him down with rough pats and wipes, without meeting his eyes or showing any expression or touching his face. Then she elbows him across the room towards a white cabinet, repeating a word he doesn't understand. Opening and shutting drawers, she selects the appropriate prophylactic. Then she orders him on to the operating table.

AFTER the earthquake, while Pond sleeps, there is a sudden convulsion, a force, which shakes him and then squeezes the breath out of him. Is it an after-shock? A dream? A seizure? He feels no pain, just a crushing guilty exhaustion which sends him immediately back to sleep.

On waking properly he feels almost normal. The smell of *Eau Sauvage* fills the room. He showers again, dresses and goes down to breakfast. He considers using the stairs in case of another earthquake, but a sign saying *Elevator* in English confronts him so he obeys it. His back is sore from the fall in the shower. Otherwise there is no specific ache. His head is clear; there are no blank spots in his memory.

HE is waiting for a taxi to the airport. The cab doesn't turn up and he begins to panic. Why does this always happen? Taxis are not dependable on the North Shore. The plane leaves soon for Tokyo. Qantas agrees to hold the plane, but only after he mentions names, the mining industry, the fact that it is a government-backed delegation, Japanese trade, a reception to be given by the Japanese Prime Minister and so forth. Qantas says thirty minutes only.

Beth has to drive him and she is in a state. The traffic is sluggish all the way from Wahroonga. He is edgy; Beth's face is stony but tearful. Unsaid sentences hang in the air: he is always going away, the marriage is over. At the airport she turns her mouth from his kiss.

Inside the terminal, despite the rush, he telephones Beth's mother. 'Keep an eye on her,' he says. He is suddenly worried that she might do something. Airline staff shuffle and look at their watches. Economy and business classes have long since boarded. It isn't clear to him that he will see Beth again.

IT'S a long time since the certainties of his days as a mining engineer. Life was based on precision. Now he is 'management', on the board, and everything is on the verge of unreality. The old engineering phrase *angle of repose* occurs often to him these days. He feels he is living at the maximum angle at which he can exist without sliding.

Things are always on edge, about to tip. Beth, who took it badly when Matthew dropped out of university after only five weeks, takes it worse when he leaves home. She takes it even harder when he hitches north and joins the Hare Krishnas. In no time it is more than just another phase, more than his surfing craze or his post-punk fad or his alternative-farming thing. In no time he has become an initiated 'devotee' and taken a Hare Krishna name which Pond can't bring himself to remember. During their rare conversations he still calls him Matt.

Now Matthew lives mostly in Queensland. When his father phones him the people who answer are politely vague about his whereabouts. Northern New South Wales, they think. Or maybe Darwin. Pond imagines them not passing on his messages. He imagines them hiding behind brocade curtains stifling giggles.

Suddenly people with shaved heads and pony tails begin jigging around the edges of his consciousness. In the street he often hears cymbals and drums in the distance. On city corners he looks for Matthew among the ointment-faced chanters and stompers and then looks away in case he sees him.

Matthew has described his new life as 'moving around a lot, preaching'. Pond finds it hard to imagine his shy and sensitive son 'preaching'. To whom, the other converted? Beth is sure he has ruined his life;

Matthew insists he has saved it. Either way, Beth cries every day and seems to hold her husband responsible.

EVENTUALLY they have little more to say on the subject of Matthew. Gradually they stop talking about other painful topics as well. Pond dreads returning to her cold tearful face of an evening. Occasionally a late meeting or an early flight are an excuse to stay in town overnight, at Tattersall's or even the Hilton. It becomes a habit. There is a brief fling with a woman from the office, but she transfers to Melbourne.

ON Christmas Eve Matthew phones out of the blue. He is in Sydney on his way somewhere. He might call around tomorrow. That night his parents are so excited and nervous they can't sleep. In his study Pond has a photograph of his son, aged five, sitting on the lowest branch of the jacaranda in the garden, smiling at the camera with his baby teeth. He — the photographer — hadn't noticed the bull ants swarming up the tree. Matthew was stung on the thigh seconds after he took the shot.

On Christmas Eve, unable to sleep, Pond is reading in the study and he glances up suddenly at Matthew about to be stung, happy, at that frozen instant, but about to cry in pain, and he loses his breath, feels an iron bar pressing on his throat. Choking, he weeps to save himself and is surprised at the relief of tears.

WHEN Matthew arrives by taxi next morning there are more surprises. He is taller, fit-looking and politely

154

smiling. There is no odd haircut, no clay markings on his face. His clothes are more conservative than his father's. He carries a briefcase. He looks like a North Shore parent's dream son, or an insurance salesman from 1954.

'That's their latest ruse,' Beth whispers in the kitchen. 'Looking normal.'

Matthew sits in an armchair like a visiting uncle and opens their presents, carefully chosen for their inoffensiveness. He has no presents for them. They wait earnestly for him to reveal his divine afflatus and they laugh at anything approaching a joke. But their son has run out of slang and forgotten old memories. His epiphany seems to have been little more than the joy of Asian lacto-vegetarianism. His talk is of dhal and ghee, the perfect papadom, his voice becoming softer and softer until it stops altogether. He politely pats the dog of his childhood. He flips in a scholarly way through the magazine rack, frowning at garish *Time* and *Vogue*. He peers in the fridge and says, 'Gee, you've got *fruit* in here!'

His parents are conscious of behaving unnaturally but can't help themselves. Beth has a secret cigarette going in the kitchen and she can't stop fidgeting and running back and forth to Matthew with fruity and nutty delicacies. He picks at them suspiciously. Perched on the edge of his chair making conversation, Pond feels like the candidate for a job that has already been filled. He is looking for some sign from this detached young man. Of familiarity, intimacy. Memory would do; he'd be happy with a recognition of past events, of the bull ants on the jacaranda, of Christmases past.

Matthew smiles indulgently at their cups of caffeine, frowns at his watch, picks up his briefcase and softly says goodbye.

THE censors have attacked all the cover girls in the bookshop. Not only the *Playboy* and *Penthouse* bunnies and pets but also the clothed and aloof *Vogue*, *Elle* and *Vanity Fair* models have ugly black smears across their chests and pelvises.

The nuances of Japanese culture are lost on Pond this morning. But at least the Imperial Hotel bookshop hasn't hedged on the central dilemma — the sword is just as evident as the chrysanthemum. He is browsing along the shelves after breakfast, waiting for his companions to assemble in the lobby. The range of books on Mishima's act of harakiri takes up as much shelf space as the ikebana picture books.

HIS mother's image of Japan is of cherry blossom branches and raked gravel. Perhaps envisioning a serene suburban widowhood spent handfeeding the carp in her kimono, she is attempting to create the vision in her garden at Lane Cove. She has planted miniature bamboo and dug a fish pond. She has bought a truck-load of river pebbles and laid down plastic sheeting to smother the weeds. But unkempt Australia overwhelms the harmony of Nippon. Crows eat the goldfish, while the delicate bamboo indecently thrives, immediately mutating into something thick and coarse, stretching up to the sun and down to the neighbours' sewage pipes.

It is only since his father's death that she feels free to

indulge her interest in Japan. His father flew Boston bombers against the Japanese in New Guinea. As his mother grows older and more sentimental she increasingly mentions how brave and dashing he was, her Flight-Lieutenant, how decorated, although he can't recall any such complimentary references while his father was alive.

HIS father mentions the war only once that he can remember and even this reference is indirect. He is recalling his old flying school days at Point Cook, Victoria. He names a couple of friends. 'We were all pilots later in New Guinea,' he says. He pauses. Will he go on? 'Three Bostons flew into this cloudbank over Wewak. Only one flew out of it.'

But he has his revenge on the economic front. For thirty-five years his father maintains a personal boycott of Japanese products. He deliberately fails to purchase a Toyota or Nissan. (He drives Fords through thick and thin.) Forget Sanyo, he wilfully watches and listens to HMV. When he becomes sick there is a family joke: 'Let's spring it on him now that his pacemaker was made in Japan.'

THE air-raid shelter behind the lantana hedge in the back yard: by 1952 it is an underground hideout full of spiders. But it is still a mine of Japanese intelligence. Shored up with war comics, souvenirs and *The Knights of Bushido*. One boy has a Japanese sword, one a pistol holster, another an officer's cap from Singapore. Tales of torture, treachery and obsession. Pearl Harbour. The Burma Railroad. Prison camp executioners.

Insane kamikazes. The idea of these manic airmen, grinning human bombs, sends its special thrill of terror through the boys. *Banzai!*

IN the hotel bookshop Pond's eyes are drawn to a book on the kamikazes. It's a collection of their last letters, translated into English, called *Voices from the Sea*. The boy in the air-raid shelter eagerly buys it and stuffs it in his briefcase.

HE learns that the literal translation of *kamikaze* is *heavenly wind* and that the term acquired its emotive meaning in the thirteenth century. Kublai Khan, grandson of Genghis Khan, had already overthrown the Sung dynasty and conquered China, as well as Turkestan, Manchuria, Korea, Annam and Burma. In 1281 he demanded that Japan too should surrender to him. Japan refused the barbarian's request. Kublai Khan ordered 100,000 warriors and 3,000 ships to conquer Japan. But the Mongols were slaphappy sailors and the enthusiasm of their Chinese and Korean auxiliaries was only lukewarm. The fleet sailed at the height of the typhoon season and, in sight of the Japanese coast, was destroyed in a storm. The *kamikaze*, the *heavenly wind*, had saved the Empire of the Rising Sun.

In spite of the heavenly wind, MacArthur is to be a luckier barbarian than Kublai Khan.

IT was after the disastrous Philippines air and naval battle that Vice-Admiral Onishi came up with the idea of using voluntary pilots who had taken a vow of suicide. His scheme was taken up by Tokyo's General Staff as a means of inflicting heavy losses on the American fleet while stirring a despairing population at home with visions of sacrifice and romance.

The kamikazes were made a special corps with their own chief, Vice-Admiral Ugaki, and a distinctive uniform: on the tunic seven buttons decorated with three petals of cherry blossom, on the sleeve the anchor of the navy. A big fuss was made of them — and of their families at home, who were given the title 'Very Honorable'. It was important that a kamikaze's mind should be free of worry about his family.

The people of Japan were told of the kamikazes' existence by special communiqué issued by General Staff headquarters in November 1944. The story of the 'hero-gods' was immediately taken up by the press and then the people.

The official instructions given to the first kamikaze corps pointed out that the Empire stood at the crossroads between victory and defeat. The first suicide unit, triumphing through the power of the spirit, would inspire others to follow its example.

The instructions went on: 'It is out of the question for you to return alive. Your mission involves certain death. Your bodies will be dead, but not your spirits. The death of a single one of you will be the birth of a million others. Neglect nothing that may affect your training or your health. You must not leave behind you any cause for regret which would follow you into eternity.'

*   *   *

MR UEDA of Tanabe Steel ushers them from the first day's meetings to dinner and then to a men's drinking club, the Big Joy Club. The club has little Australian flags on the bar, and framed photographs of a koala and a frill-necked lizard. The professionally flirtatious hostesses pour them continual glasses of Suntory whisky and bully everyone into singing a song. Pond renders a desultory version of *Waltzing Matilda*. Back at the hotel, although drunk and tired, he is too restless to sleep and stays up reading *Voices from the Sea*.

MOST of the 'hero-gods' were recruited from the universities of Tokyo and Kyoto. Secret instructions from the General Staff had recommended that the corps should take either the worst pilots or the youngest ones who had not yet undergone full training. The others, the professionals, were essential for the defence of Japan.

These younger and less capable pilots were given old aircraft which had been stripped of most of their armaments and instruments. They were given only enough fuel for the flight to their target, and they were escorted there by fighters. Their orders were to crash-land on their targets — battleships or, preferably, aircraft carriers.

ON the eve of their departure the student pilots were given a funeral banquet. They were dressed in white, the colour of mourning. They symbolically divested themselves of all their worldly goods. They were each given a little white box in which to place cuttings of their hair and fingernails, to be sent to their family to be placed on the family altar in place of their ashes.

Sometimes the last night of the kamikazes degenerated into an orgy. Many of them got drunk on sake to keep their spirits up. Often they were provided with women from the villages around the air base. Even drunk and sated they were rarely able to sleep.

POND drinks more whisky while he reads, every now and then getting up and dashing water on his face and pacing around the room before returning to the book.

The pilots' letters are mainly in the form of diary entries. One young law student admitted that he wasn't dying voluntarily. 'I am not going to my death without severe regrets,' he wrote. Next day he crashed his aircraft into the sea off Okinawa. No American shipping was nearby.

Another boy wrote proudly that he had just passed his basic flying test. 'I did the test at 7.40. I was very touched as I walked out of the hangar to see the mechanics fussing around my machine. It was a bright morning, the ceiling was at 6,000 feet. I flew round and round for a long time and I enjoyed it in spite of everything.'

Next day this boy's orders came. 'I take off tomorrow morning,' he wrote. 'Tonight the electric light has failed in my room. Oil burns in a tin and the flame throws shadows against the wall. Next door they are rowdy, playing gramophone records and drinking spirits. They probably have the right idea but I prefer to wait quietly.'

He farewelled his parents and asked them to pray for him. 'Twenty-three years of life are approaching their end,' he said. 'I am biting my fingers and the tears are flowing. With my eyes closed I evoke Mother's beloved image. She will never leave me.'

And then he wrote: 'A breath of wind arises. The Kamikaze. It comes to sweep away the sadness of my heart. I write the word "tomorrow" and stare at it. My life will have no tomorrow. My heart has no deviations. You will not receive my ashes; I will substitute my fingernails and my hair.'

AFTER reading the boy's farewell Pond's head spins. The boy's night-light flickers in his mind and his heart races with sympathy and fatigue. The trails of aftershave lingering in the room sting his senses and make him nauseous and thirsty. He drinks a glass of water and tastes chemicals. Pacing the room, he feels alternately drunk and sober and is only slightly surprised to find himself suddenly on his back on the carpet.

Seconds or minutes pass. The cracks in the ceiling remind him of the rosy broken veins which appeared in the cheeks of Mr Ueda of Tanabe Steel while Mr Ueda was singing, in alternate Japanese and English, *Love Me Tender*. Mr Ueda's romantic intensity and rosy cheeks were not evident during their protracted negotiations earlier in the day. Mr Ueda didn't have a sentimental bone in his body at 3 pm, but at midnight his eyes brimmed. He had his own drink locker at the Big Joy Club and his hostess smacked his cheeky hands and combed his hair for him in front of everyone.

Pond the engineer wonders whether the cracks are old or new. Eventually, making a decision, he gets up and moves to the telephone. Concentrating intently, he makes a call to Beth in Sydney. There is no answer.

Then he moves to the window, resting his forehead against the glass and peering down on the bright malls and intersections of the business district. Bright signs flash for Seiko and Honda and Sanyo, and far off there is a neon champagne glass with popping bubbles.

And the window pane bumps against his head — two, three, four times. *Oh, Beth. Oh, Matt*. For a second his chest caves in like an accordion. When his breath comes back he knows he must leave the building, flee the earthquake. He hurries out of the swaying room, down the stairs, seven flights, and through the lobby into the street.

At the curb a taxi waits, quite motionless. The hotel is immobile again and everywhere Pond looks all the building lines remain straight and angles are secure at ninety degrees. The city, the night itself, is also still. Hazy clouds cover the stars and the moon is a faint milky light.

Pond concentrates on adjusting his thinking. He tries to test the earth's mood and intentions with the soles of his feet. Back and forth he paces in front of the hotel, searching the skyline. Finally he spots the neon champagne glass. Keeping it strictly in view he signals the cab and points it out to the driver.

'Take me to that glass,' he says.

The driver is impassively reading a sex comic. He tears his eyes away to glance vaguely in the direction of the glass, then demands to be paid first. Pond gives him a handful of notes and they set off. Perhaps ten minutes later the cab stops, Pond climbs out and the cab accelerates away.

The buildings are too high for him to find the champagne glass; it's impossible to guess if its bubbles pop above him or not. But across the pavement there is a bar or restaurant displaying the usual plastic replicas of the food available inside: canny likenesses of sushi and shavings of fat-marbled beef and perfectly crafted slices of okra and seaweed and individual grains of rice. And sake, beer and whisky bottles.

Pond pushes at the door. When it resists him he begins thumping. Soon he hears footsteps and a short, thickset man comes to the door, taps his watch and waves him away. When Pond produces a wad of money the man punches his fist threateningly into his palm.

Pond backs away from the door. As he stands indecisively in the street three men meander towards him, two of them steering and supporting a smaller drunken one whose cheeks, like Mr Ueda's, shine like cherries. They are all wearing business suits and, as they pass, the small man, inevitably, shouts abuse.

One of the more sober men mutters an apology. He is so contrite, bowing slightly, that Pond begins to ask him about the neon champagne glass's whereabouts and, lacking language, mimes the act of drinking. Abruptly the drunken man brushes off his helpers and lurches over to him. His head comes to Pond's chest and his affronted oiled hair rises in a porcupine's spikes. The ground is trembling beneath them; Pond's arms fly out to balance himself against the tremors and immediately the drunk exhales a sour whisky yell and lunges at him.

Caught in the chest, Pond sits down hard. As the spiky-haired man reels above him roaring joyous gibberish, the earth shudders and re-forms itself.

*   *   *

164

WILL he and the earth ever stabilise? Taking light and steady breaths, focusing on each action and small accomplishment, he finds that it matters less.

He gets to the nearest intersection and hails a cab. It knows where he is going. At the brothel, in the dream-dentist's waiting room, the mama-san is watching cartoons with the old man. They chuckle without sounds, the laughter compressed into their foreheads and upper lips. A chubby rabbit teases a skinny fox. Both animals are dressed as farmers, in checked shirts and overalls. The rabbit gooses the fox with a pitch-fork. Apparently this jab is the latest in a stream of barnyard indignities because the fox chases the rabbit and decapitates him with an axe. The TV color is rich and accurate tonight. Blood spurts from the rabbit's neck-stump; he flops around in dripping circles like a chicken. But there are no cartoon miracles in this place. Bunny's head doesn't pop back as cheeky as ever; the eyes on the severed head roll back; the ears go limp. It's curtains for bunny.

Pond looks at his watch; it's later than he imagined. *Ahem*. He stands up and taps the watch face. The old couple look keenly at him; their grim hesitation is a statement. Finally the mama-san gets up from her chair and pads out of the room. Pond calls after her, hoarse beseeching English hanging in the air: 'Could I have a woman who kisses?'

The shame strikes him at once. The old man turns abruptly back to the television, which is all greens and purples again. Again a game show is taking place. Toothy young men in running-shoes spring about with clipboards under their arms. Purple smiling hos-tesses move like robots, clutching burning tapers in

165

their talons. Again the line of shuffling males appears, this time ten or twelve of them, company men identically dressed in mauve business suits. Their expressions are serious as they touch their toes; their trouser seats tauten as the camera pans over them and a hostess fussily tucks their jackets out of the way. And then another hostess passes behind them, coy as any magician's assistant, and waves her taper-wand behind each trouser seat.

The old man's chuckling escapes his closed mouth and rises high in his throat. One by one the bending men break wind. The hostess's taper flares and fizzes and individual flames shoot out across the screen.

Once again it is the woman with the nurse's demeanour who sullenly beckons him into her antiseptic, steaming room. He welcomes her like an old friend. Nevertheless, a moment later, his special request is denied.

HIS hotel stands solidly on its foundations. This is a satisfactory discovery. Pond is relieved to be walking through the lobby of the Imperial. Going up to his room, entering it, he feels that to an extent he is home and this calms him even more. Slowly and methodically he showers and shaves. He even cuts his fingernails and, with the nail scissors, trims his hair in the front where it isn't so grey. He dresses in clean clothes and packs all his belongings in his suitcase.

On hotel stationery he writes a letter to Beth and Matthew and places the cuttings of his hair and fingernails in the envelope. He takes the letter down to the front desk and returns to the security of his room.

166

Then he lies on the bed, and after thinking for a long while of Beth and Matthew, of life-stages and times when they were all younger, he begins to concentrate on the vibrations passing through and around his body. He is open to all the tremors and changes of the external and internal worlds. He feels all the movements along the fault plane as the daylight gradually comes through the window of his room.

THE HAMMETT SPIEL

RIGHT away I tell my tour groups that if things had gone a little differently for Dashiell Hammett an enduring American legend would not have begun and *Australia* might have given birth to the hard-boiled private eye.

Australia, that's right. Unthinkable. It'd be like losing the cowboy to Norway or somewhere. 'Events,' I say, 'might have turned out a shade differently for Lillian Hellman, too.' They smile at this. They're good-natured and savvy, the people who enjoy hard-boiled detective stories.

So, this was Hammett's situation in 1921: he'd just been discharged, a bit frail, from a TB sanitorium. He'd recently married one of his nurses. And he'd gone back to work for Pinkerton's in San Francisco. The TB had started him toying with the idea of changing his life. He was twenty-seven and keen to become a writer.

'Just about my age,' I tell my tour groups, standing on the steps of City Hall in my fedora and open trench coat, flashing a glimpse of my Maltese Falcon tie. I know the get-up's corny, but they like it and it helps them to distinguish me from the various dispirited ratepayers, winos, optimistic gays and eccentrics who congregate on the steps. Two pm Wednesday and

171

Saturday; five dollars a head and anything up to thirty in a group. Mind you, that's tops and wet days it's zilch. The money's not really important, anyway. I have this knowledge and I might as well share it. Hammett's my interest.

My room mate June kind of understands but yet she doesn't. Her own fascination is for local women authors. She did a course on them at Berkeley. Ina D. Coolbrith. Gertrude Atherton. Virginia Rath. June reads only women authors as a point of principle. She's narrowing it down to only those within a fifty-mile radius. Los Angeles is definitely out. She gets to read a lot on night shift up at the Kaiser Hospital. When someone gives me an investigation assignment it's usually a night one — surveillance work and so on — so our lifestyles don't clash.

While I'm waiting for latecomers to join the group on the steps my spiel goes that Hammett was beginning to write snatches of verse, small sketches of detective life and bits of stories when he got one of his biggest assignments.

Some two hundred thousand in gold bullion — a big sum in 1921 — was missing from an Australian ship that had docked in San Francisco. The insurance company employed the Pinkerton Agency to find the gold, which they believed was still stashed away on the boat. Hammett and another operative were sent to search the ship — and found nothing. So the insurance company decided to send Hammett back to Australia on the ship in the belief that he might still find the missing loot.

Now, from my reading, and from interviewing several old colleagues of his including, significantly, a former barkeep at John's Grill, I believe that at this stage of his life Hammett was not only looking forward to the adventure but saw it as a chance to start afresh in Australia. As you know, it's a raw, remote, healthy country — a sort of Last Frontier — and this appealed to him.

But he was a real professional, and until the ship sailed he felt bound to keep searching for the gold. Just before it left he made a last routine search and found the gold hidden in a smokestack. He had solved the case and lost his trip to Australia. Annoyed and frustrated by his success, he handed his resignation to Pinkerton's, moved away from his wife into a cheap single room and began to write seriously.

An interesting observation I've made after two or three hundred Dashiell Hammett Tours: at this point the men in the group invariably nod understandingly, their eyes warm and full of sympathy. The women show no expression at all. They have momentarily forgotten the love story that they adore — the long, romantic Hammett-Hellman relationship that endured all: chronic illness, alcohol, the McCarthy purges, prison — even the loss of his talent and the corresponding blossoming of hers. At the moment they're thinking: confused sad wife, severance of secure job, uncertain bohemian existence looming, stray women, booze. I can see it twice a week in their suddenly expressionless eyes.

And these aren't your typical Fisherman's Wharf *turistas*. Most of them are locals. Last Saturday I had a *Playboy* cartoonist, a science fiction novelist, and a woman who did her Ph.D. on 'The Proto-Marxist Influence of Dashiell Hammett on American Literature'. From her I learned that *The Maltese Falcon* was really the history of capitalism, something about the falcon itself being an item of plunder, what Marx called 'the primitive accumulation'.

'When its gold and gems were painted over,' the Ph.D. explained, 'it became a mystified object, a piece of property that belonged to no-one. Whoever possessed it didn't really own it.'

We were drinking in the Market Street bar that I generally repair to after the tour, a more or less authentic Hammett-style joint where you can get a shot of California whiskey and a beer chaser for $2.25 from kindly old silver-haired White Russian bartenders. Pre-Earthquake city scenes line the walls, and portraits of early stout fire chiefs and sheriffs. The customers are elderly and weary and both sexes wear hats. Occasionally a tour member loses a wallet or a purse there, but by this time they're exhausted from three hours' trudging around various Hammett addresses in the Tenderloin, Chinatown, Russian Hill and downtown and, full of my spiel, are generally regarding crime in a nostalgic light.

The Hammett Ph.D., excitedly downing her chaser first, reminded me that the falcon statuette was at the same time another fiction, a work of art which turned out itself to be a fake, actually made of lead.

'Hammett's whole world was fraudulent, equivocal, sexist and brutally acquisitive,' she went on. She was interesting-looking, twenty-eightish, with clean-smelling straight hair and green eyes. She volunteered that she was a librarian at the public library. 'I have an apartment down the road at 580 McAllister Street,' she said.

I took this partly as the hopeful statement of availability of the San Francisco heterosexual female, partly as the remark of a fellow Hammett buff. Of course 580 McAllister was the address of The Whosis Kid, from the story of the same name. It was where The Continental Op shadowed him, was captured, and where he finally shot The Kid dead — 'arms spread in a crucified posture'.

'You should've mentioned it when we stopped at your place on the tour,' I told her. 'When I stood there ranting on your doorstep.'

'I didn't want to steal your thunder.'

'Dames!' I said, tipping my hat back on my head.

'Your hat kills me,' she said, leaning across and flicking its brim.

'Got any booze at your place?' I asked. 'I've never actually been inside 580 McAllister. It's a gap in my knowledge.'

'They've tidied it up since they carted The Kid out,' the Ph.D. said, staring hard-boiledly at me across the table.

VARIOUS bums were slinking around the front of 580 McAllister when we arrived — the usual junkies, dipsos and crazy desperates. A fat prostitute whizzed through the broken glass on roller skates. I patted my left armpit and they made way for us. I don't actually carry a gun; they're not giving out any more concealed-weapon licences these days. But in San Francisco I look cop enough to get by. The cops in this town are all show ponies: handlebar moustaches, snakeskin boots, shaved heads, alligator loafers. Compared to them I blend into the landscape.

175

In the Ph.D.'s apartment we drank white wine under hanging fern baskets and discussed Sam Spade and Co. Hammett of course gave Spade his actual apartment at 891 Post Street, on Hyde, where he was writing *The Maltese Falcon* in 1928. I guess it made things easier creatively.

Undeniably on the premises of 580 McAllister, I could, by a stretch of the imagination, see myself as The Continental Op and her as the exotic Ines Almad, jewel thief and manipulator of men. The Continental Op was standoffish to women, however, whereas I am not.

While I was playing with this image she disappeared, slightly self-consciously, into the bedroom. I smiled to myself. Dum-de-dum-dum. I browsed nonchalantly through a pile of magazines on her coffee table. *The New York Review of Books*. Huh-hmm. *Ms* magazine. *Gun World*. The Ph.D. was a woman of surprises. 'Low Bucks Protection! New Rossi Revolvers!' blurbed *Gun World*. 'Big-Bore for Bad Guys — Ithaca Mag-10 Roadblocker!' yelled *Gun World*. On the wall above the coffee table was a portrait of Kafka, beloved of librarians, and a Save-the-Whale poster. I found these more in character.

Three or four minutes passed. I looked at my watch. I had a surveillance job at 8 pm at the futon warehouse on Folsom Street. They wanted me to watch the nightwatchman, suspected of pilfering a futon a week. He was a Vietnamese, hard to pin down to a definite timetable of movements. It was now 6.30 — I still had a half hour before I'd have to race home, change and grab a bite. Maybe June had left one of her garbanzo bean casseroles or stuffed eggplants in the oven. June is a vegetarian. I ride with it at home, I respect her beliefs, but I spread the perimeter of our relationship when I'm out. Like, when I lose torque after eight hours outside a motel or whatever, I head straight for McDonald's.

'How're you doing in there, baby?' I called.

From the bedroom came a surge of stereo sound. Heavy-breathy disco, black girls panting and singing high in their heads. My taste runs to Hoagie Carmichael. *Buttermilk Sky* and so forth. It's not nostalgia — I wasn't even born then — I'm just a romantic. That's how I got into this private investigation business in the first place.

I carried my wine to the bedroom door and looked in. The Ph.D. was lying back on a high brass bed, palely naked and beckoning.

'Come here,' she said.

'Sure.'

'Discard your costume,' she ordered.

Still smiling cutely, she turned the stereo volume up even higher so the speakers on either side of the bed throbbed like an amplified pulse. Then she reached under the pillow and pulled out a Smith and Wesson, model 39, and pointed it at me.

'I shoot sharpshooter quality,' she said, one professional to another. 'Not that it matters at this range.'

As I was struggling with my shoelaces, she remarked conversationally, 'I always have a grudging respect for the person who commits a crime with a classy weapon — even if it's stolen. Saturday night specials are an affront aesthetically, if nothing else.'

'Indeed,' I murmured. I cleared my throat.

'There's a new .380 Beretta that I've got my eye

177

on — a straight blowback that slap-loads thirteen rounds ...'

I finished undressing. The Ph.D. cocked the Smith and Wesson.

'Now you better make it good, shamus.'

Hammett's first job for Pinkerton's, I recalled, concentrating deeply, churning my spiel through my head, was to trace a fellow who stole a ferris wheel from a carnival. He tracked him up to Oregon and arrested him but the guy escaped. With the ferris wheel.

THE BAY OF
CONTENTED MEN

The Hong Kong Album

SALLY said that Vincent was in Stanley Prison, just up the hill, for 'some white-collar crime'.

'So — you'll need to find another apartment when he gets out,' Andrea said to her as they headed down the hill towards the tiny lights bobbing on the beach.

'Oh, I don't think so,' Sally said, and laughed her skittish laugh. The laugh, the glint in her eyes, hinted that she wasn't herself, or was too much herself, at the moment.

Vincent owned Sally's apartment back on Stanley Beach Road where, at her urging, Ed and Andrea had stopped only long enough to drop off their bags and change into swimming costumes. Sally said she'd never met Vincent but the note in her laugh reminded Andrea, still giddy from the flight and the temperature change, of a certain mood of Sally's from her Green Dwarf period.

Possibly due to the influence of her father, an astronomer knighted for discovering changes to the color index of stars, Sally gave her men nicknames to do with colors. The Green Dwarf had come before the Black Knave and the White Prince, but his nickname said as much about her own self-image as her feelings for him.

181

The Green Dwarf was short and slight, with the same fair-haired, green-eyed, almost translucent pallor as herself. They could have been twins. Andrea remembered him as a bossy and successful merchant banker (and less successful film investor) apt to say 'Sally is my kind of woman' without a trace of humor, and 'Ciao' on departing. His hold on Sally and her skittish laugh had ended only on his writing her a 'letter of comfort' setting out his intentions for them, or her — that she give up the theatre for marriage and children — which he signed off with his jaunty Ciao. He spelled it C.H.O.W. Her repugnance at the letter of comfort had palled beside the realisation that the Green Dwarf had been thinking and saying Chow to her every day for two years.

Like the air, the water at Stanley Beach was almost at body temperature. But the bottom was firm and not too slimy underfoot. On the shoreline, even at this late hour, children and parents crouched over glowing toys, little lantern-boats, while behind them on the dry sand grandmothers sat on mats holding candles.

There could be anything in that tepid black water. 'What's the shark situation?' asked Ed.

'They're all in the soup,' Sally laughed.

'What about pollution?'

Sally laughed again and strode into the bay. She had lost more weight in Hong Kong. Her gleaming shoulder blades stuck out sharply; her thighs seemed not to meet. It was a funny place to be a theatre administrator; only someone on the run from the White Prince would consider it. Andrea and Ed followed her into the bay.

'You have to swim out to the raft,' Sally ordered. She

plunged in first and came up squealing, as if she were thirteen and it was her first swim of the season back at Lorne or Apollo Bay, as if it weren't bathwater-warm but the nipping surf of the Southern Ocean. She backstroked out into the bay and in the dark her grinning teeth showed for a long moment.

For forty or fifty metres Ed swam after her, stroking into the pinpricks of lights from islands and fishing junks. The bay became darker and deeper but the raft stayed out of reach, a blurry bulge on the distant surface. Colder currents trailed across his legs when he rested but his face felt feverish.

Andrea called for them to wait. She was puffing and spluttering as she caught up and rested on Ed's shoulder. 'Darling, why are we doing this?'

He was disoriented, with a sore throat from the flight. He didn't fancy swallowing any of this unlikely seawater that skidded off the skin and made him sweat. He called to Sally, 'That's enough for us!'

'Pikers!' Sally turned and backstroked into shore. As they dried themselves she was huffy. They hadn't kept to her itinerary. But then she rallied and gave a beaming smile. 'It's so *wonderful* to see you,' she said.

She had obviously gone to some trouble for their visit. Back at the apartment she had a redfish waiting to bake. The air-conditioner was cooling their bedroom, wine was chilling, and while they showered she put out bowls of nuts and prawn crackers. 'It's so *special* having you here,' she said. 'I'm so *honoured*.'

Ed opened the duty-free Tanqueray and they drank gin and tonics while the fish cooked. Muddy sweet smells rose from the garden. Spicy cooking odours came from somewhere nearby, and women's voices

singing snatches of pop songs. The living room over-
looked the bay; above the window a gecko gripped the
ceiling. All around the room unfamiliar plants with
shiny leaves trailed over surfaces. Andrea tied her hair
up from her neck and lit a cigarette. She leaned back in
her chair, bare feet up on the coffee table, lifted her
skirt and fanned air up her thighs.

'Well, the tropics,' she said.

'Absolutely,' Sally said.

'I love it,' said Andrea, waving her arms and shooting
glances all around. 'All this.' She spotted something.
'Oh, God, where did you get that lamp?'

The lamp on the coffee table in front of her was
shaped like a pair of breasts.

Sally gave her laugh. 'That's Vincent's.' She explained that the apartment had become available, completely stocked and furnished, when Vincent went to
jail six months before. Apparently Vincent came from
the Seychelles and was a 'consultant'. Sally rented the
apartment from one of his friends, an English girl who
called around every fortnight for the rent and mail.

'I'm worried about his American Express bills,' Sally
said. 'I don't think Fiona's paying them on time.' She
giggled. 'You know how cross they get.'

While they drank gin and waited for dinner, Sally
filled them in on her recent exploits. An annual round-
the-world ticket went with her job — a brief visit home
to Melbourne, then on to New York and London. The
theatre had been disappointing in all these cities but
Sally was philosophical. In New York a team of black
security men had burst into her room at the Algonquin
at midnight when the steam from her hot shower set
off the fire alarm. 'Very exciting,' Sally said. Her first

thought had been to remove her shower cap, thinking it unflattering, but after wrenching the alarm off the wall the men backed out of the bathroom with their hatchets and extinguishers and tool belts and were out in the corridor, clanking and giggling, within minutes. And in London she'd flirted with a Ugandan mini-cab driver who told her Idi Amin had murdered his family. She was sympathetic. When she got out of the cab in Chelsea he squeezed her hand and gave her his phone number. Later that night, after two vodkas, she rang the number but it was false.

So the only man she'd collared in New York or London this time had been the Black Knave, resting at the Heathrow Hilton between flights and conferences. He was 'too tired' to come to her in Chelsea so she went to him. Twenty pounds each way in the taxi, 'but it was worth it,' even though the trip back with the Ugandan came to nothing more than Walton Street.

Oh, on British Airlines between Kennedy and Heathrow she *was* propositioned by a papery old man who coughed blood politely into a handkerchief and offered her musk Life Savers. His card said *Mr Gordon Pynt, Teacher, Ballroom Dancing* and gave the address of a residential hotel on the Lower East Side. 'I have a little bundle saved for my regular visit to London. I am of British descent myself,' he said. When he wasn't coughing he was limping to the toilet. 'My dear, may I remark on your marvellous bearing?' he said to Sally. He hawked gently and his lips extruded a bloody musk ring on to his handkerchief. 'I presume you dance?' Sally patted his wrist. 'I earnestly hope we can liaise in London,' said Mr Gordon Pynt. 'Darling, you're sweet,' said Sally. 'And now I must shut my eyes for an hour or two.'

185

With their gins Sally played one of Vincent's records. Crystal Gayle. 'I like it,' she said rather defensively. '"Your Cheatin' Heart" and so on.'

ON the first available evidence Vincent is slender, beige-skinned, almond-eyed, a lithe and dapper mixture of several races. He seems self-conscious and narcissistic. He frequents gaudy nightclubs. He's either very fond of women's company — especially showgirls — or he likes being photographed with them.

There is a difference, Ed thinks, but on the evidence — the photographs in the thick maroon album which Sally has placed in his hands — it's not clear which is the case.

Ed is content pondering the question. He's pleased to be in Hong Kong, to be holidaying with Andrea en route to London, to be gazing across the dark bay, to be drinking gin and tonic and, above all, to be in that particular state of discarded responsibility and receptive fatigue where ideas can insinuate themselves.

Ed's personality thrives on changed and strange circumstances. He likes mysteries. Both professionally and domestically he often seems to be the fulcrum of tumult. When the dust has settled he enjoys mulling over the dramas and quirks of his life and trying to fashion them into projects. He's a director of TV commercials who is trying to make the leap to feature films. At the moment he feels his perception is heightened, as always, by travel and unfamiliar surroundings and the chance of unusual things happening to him.

He hopes a project will present itself very soon. He tells everyone, 'What I'm looking for is a good love story. A script that's romantic but unsentimental. Something with a nervy edge to it, adventurous, but with a life-affirmative ending.' (He's not courting commercial disaster; he's got to raise *money* for this.) Here he shakes his head sorrowfully. 'Tell me why this is such a tall order?'

Tonight he likes the idea of the film director (him) and the actress (Andrea), new lovers, holidaying in an exotic location with an absent criminal playing host to them.

What could he have happen next?

'Wasn't he a sweet little boy?' Sally says abruptly.

The first photograph shows a pretty little Seychellois in white shirt and short pants, his hands clasped piously before him. In the next picture he holds the Bible like a banner.

'False pretences,' Ed murmurs.

Maybe it's his first communion. Surrounding this devout presentation are coconut palms, a bush of purple bougainvillea, a garden bed of raked sand and crushed sea-shells. A cement step intrudes, and the edge of a limestone church. Ed imagines a weathered Virgin, a saint or two, posing solemnly in the sun beyond the picture's frame.

Vincent's photographed childhood is brief. For an instant he's a stern twelve-year-old boy scout saluting the camera, flanked by weary-looking parents, then suddenly he's an extravagantly dressed and side-burned youth of the early seventies, all long collars and flared trousers and high-heeled boots.

This new Vincent has secrets. A smug and sullen cloud has fallen over his adolescent face. And it hasn't gained any more spontaneity. (So far there's no photo-

187

graph where his pose isn't carefully planned.) From his sulky attitude it seems inevitable that Vincent will soon be leaving the Seychelles of sunny churches and gritty gardens for more exciting backdrops. And within one page of the album his new background of garish nightclubs indicates that this has happened.

A certain insincerity, a mysterious job as a 'consultant', dishonesty (he's a convicted criminal, after all) — what other clues are there to the character of Sally's landlord? But, Ed wonders, are these really clues? Don't they depend on the morality and taste of the busybody? And aren't they colored by the busybody's knowledge that Vincent is currently doing time?

Well, there's the nightclub question. Can you trust someone who is always in nightclubs? Why not? Maybe he's a nightclub consultant. Maybe the stagily posed and tinted prints, the work of nightclub photographers, are part of his curriculum vitae. Vincent is certainly embracing a variety of exotic and suggestive entertainers. There are blonde and red-haired strippers, dark belly-dancers in harem pants and tasselled brassieres, even several high-breasted, firm-jawed showgirls who could be transvestites. All of them are fussing over him, trailing their fingers seductively over his shoulders, perching on his knees and lighting his cigarillos. While they have plenty of amusing and coquettish flounces for the camera, these are not ironic flounces. He's not a normal customer. They are not taking the mickey.

No, it's Vincent who sometimes looks as if his heart is not in it. Yes, his arms are draped familiarly around that blonde stripper, his hand hanging only centimetres from her jutting white breast, but his smile is jaded, his thoughts are elsewhere. Perhaps he's just tired after a hard night's consulting. Maybe he's just making a point like he did when he thrust the Bible at the camera fifteen, twenty, twenty-five years before. Then he wanted to be seen as a churchgoer; now he wants to be known as a nightclub-goer.

It occurs to Ed that in none of the photographs is Vincent embracing an Asian showgirl, or an Asian woman of any type. In fact, apart from a passerby in one of the outdoor shots there are no Asian women in any of the photographs.

Ed considers the odds against a Chinese woman appearing in a collection of photographs of Hong Kong showgirls. They must be considerable.

Showgirl with Plumes

WHAT could Ed have happen next in his film? It was an intriguing quandary. Somehow it revolved around Vincent. Ed and Vincent had something very much in common — the interest in showgirls. Showgirls had always held a professional fascination for Ed; he was interested in them as art, in the showgirl as a motif. Some of his best commercials over the years had sold everything from after-dinner liqueurs to medical insurance using dancers, torch singers, chorus lines, ballerinas and assorted glamorous women in nightclub settings. And his first 'legitimate' effort, ten years before, had been an experimental 60-minute 16mm film called *Showgirl with Plumes*. While he was now grateful that its only showing had been on the government TV channel at 11 pm

189

one Sunday night, he still had a soft spot for it.

The film was about a young man who fell in love with a painting of a showgirl. He was an advertising man named Ted, whose emotional state was an extreme version of his creator's (Ed's) at that particular stage of his twenty-sixth year. Ted was in a susceptible condition because of a harrowing love life and a bad series of hangovers. Ted's girlfriend Lauren, an actress (like many of Ed's over the years), was away from home shooting a commercial and he was disoriented without her.

The film's theme was anguish by art. Its impetus was partly Ed's interest in showgirls. But it was also sparked off by an article he had read in a magazine about the Stendahl Syndrome. When visiting Florence in 1817 Stendahl had been overwhelmed by frescos in the Church of Santa Croce. In his diary he later wrote of how his heart began to beat erratically, how he was near fainting, how he felt his life ebbing away. It wasn't until he left the church and sat on a bench to read the poetry of Ugo Foscolo that he began to feel better.

The syndrome had been first noted and named in the 1970s by Dr Graziella Magherini, chief of psychiatry at the Santa Maria Nuova Hospital in Florence. Suddenly, in the presence of provocative sacred paintings, sculptures or architecture, certain susceptible people — especially when far from home — broke down. Some swooned. Others began sweating profusely or experiencing rapid heart beat and stomach pains. Typically, a victim was an unmarried woman between twenty-six and forty who was travelling alone or in a small group and who was especially attracted to the Uffizi Museum. After a few days of saturating herself in the lives of the saints, the Crucifixion and the Madonna and Child she began to hallucinate, imagined she saw angels and could hear them singing. Soon she became convinced she was the reincarnation of a nun buried in a village in Umbria or somesuch. Victims tended to be from the United States.

The film began with Ted waking in his flat, alone and hungover, one Saturday morning. Slumped over the papers, his attention was caught by a story that struck him as somehow pertinent. A man had dreamed his lover was having an affair with his best friend and woke convinced the dream was real. He jumped into his car, drove to his friend's house and stabbed him in his bed with a kitchen knife.

Reading this item, Ted had the odd sensation that he had just dreamed of reading it, and living it. *Déjà rêvé*. It came as no surprise. He knew what happened next: the friend, although stabbed in the chest and stomach, rose furiously from bed and chased the dreamer-attacker outside; when the police arrived it was just dawn, before seven am, and the former friends had been fighting and moaning in the yard for half an hour; by this time they were on their knees battling with garden tools, swinging rakes and shovels at each other. A crowd of neighbours was cheering and screaming. Both men were soaked with blood and their pyjamas were in shreds.

Shortly after, Ted phoned Lauren in Alice Springs to say hello (she was shooting a perfume commercial with an Afghan camel train in central Australia), but she was out on location. Feeling lonely and in need of air, Ted went for a stroll and wandered into the State Art Gallery.

The gallery was showing an exhibition called *Old Masters, New Visions* — from El Greco to Rothko, on loan from a Washington museum. Because of its value, armed guards stood around conspicuously. Signs ordered visitors to stand behind a grey plastic strip fixed to the floor a metre from the wall, and they were obediently following this instruction, most of them viewing the paintings from a self-righteous distance a metre or so outside the line. Some shied away from the line as if it were a live electric cable which could not only frizzle them in their shoes but set off a general alarm announcing their naiveté in matters of art.

Ted stopped to peer at a painting called *Showgirl with Plumes*. It stood out in this company. The showgirl looked out of place, as if she had wandered in from a nightclub in her feathers and strapless gown and was having a boring time. Her pose was stark and frontal. Her features and flesh were night-pale, soft-looking, but her round face was hardened by fatigue and make-up. She seemed both malleable and tough. The red feathers exploded against her pallor. They heightened the delicacy of her cheek and neck and fell gently over a full white breast.

Ted stood in front of the showgirl for a long time, standing as close as he was allowed, looking into her weary, knowing eyes. Her love life is unhappy, he thought aloud. Her affair with the artist is not going well. A guided group moved in front of the painting. As if she had overheard him, the guide stepped forward and immediately tried to smother any suggestion of intimacy between artist and model.

192

'The model for *Showgirl with Plumes* — 1931, oil on canvas — probably came from an agency,' the guide announced. She was a grim, solid woman in her mid-forties. 'The artist employed many of his sitters from a particular New York theatrical booking agency, Lillies.'

Ted wondered why she was so timid and defensive about their relationship. Then the guide annoyed him further by casting around for a rationale for an artist painting a showgirl at all. 'It isn't surprising that he chose showgirls and clowns as his subject matter,' she said. 'The artist was a keen cyclist and often raced at county fairs, where he would have seen many of these characters.'

Cyclist? Clowns? Characters? Ted had never thought of showgirls as *characters*. And he envied painters. He saw painters — artists — in a shrewd but romantic light. They were bohemians. He liked the idea that a New York artist wanting to see showgirls in 1931 should have to jump on his bike and ride into the country to do so.

Ted wondered about the guide: her sophistication and knowledge of Depression America. She was dressed in a sedate blazer and check skirt. Perhaps she was trying to protect the sensibilities of school parties, old ladies, unaccustomed gallery visitors. If so, she needn't have worried. Everyone was passing by the showgirl with only a cursory glance on their way to the big-name artists, to *The Luncheon of the Boating Party* and *Entrance to the Public Gardens in Arles*. But Ted stood staring at the showgirl until it occurred to him that an indecent amount of time had passed. Two guards were looking his way. Feeling dizzy and aroused, he moved on.

In front of the Bonnards he saw an attractive woman he knew slightly gazing raptly at the paintings. She sidled up to him and said in an intimate, excited voice, 'Now I can see what everyone's been saying about the Bonnards!'

No-one had said anything to him about the Bonnards but her enthusiasm was vaguely thrilling. 'Yes,' he said.

As he stood with her frowning at the Bonnards, another attractive woman, flushed and animated, came up swiftly on his free side, nudged his arm, and, pointing to a particular Bonnard, *The Open Window*, whispered, 'That blind is actually supposed to be a guillotine.'

Ted focused on the window blind and nodded. But it looked more like a blind than a guillotine. They were standing there as an intimate threesome, he realised, with himself as the fulcrum. As he became aware of this pleasant feeling and was about to introduce them, the first woman abruptly moved off in the direction of the Cézannes. He began concentrating harder on the blind as a guillotine — and on its proximity to the trusting head of Bonnard's model — when the second woman suddenly said, 'Oh!' and sheered off towards the Renoirs. Stranded in front of the Bonnards, Ted thought he should give them a few moments longer, then he moved away.

He was drawn back to the showgirl. The artist was Walt Kuhn (American, 1877-1949). He read in his catalogue that when Walt Kuhn wasn't painting or cycling he was designing and directing musical revues, such as *The Pinwheel Revue* and *Hitchy-koo*. He was a showman too! Obviously the paths of showmen and showgirls crossed more often than those of cyclists and showgirls. How could a man who directed a show called *Hitchy-koo* not know something about showgirls?

The artist's background certainly suggested an acquaintance with nightlife. Kuhn had grown up in Red Hook, New York, in a waterfront hotel run by his German immigrant parents. He illustrated magazines in San Francisco before joining the artistic exodus to Europe where he studied painting in Paris, Munich and Berlin.

The European influence was clear to Ted. He thought the painting blended New York glamor and Old World ennui. He was struck again by the enigmatic look of the showgirl, her sexuality, the knowing absence of expression that was so much more powerful than simple American vivacity. He loved the deadpan look she was giving Walt Kuhn. *Drop dead, Walt.* He worked out that Kuhn would have been fifty-four, nearly thirty years older than himself! An old man! And the showgirl looked to be only in her early twenties!

It wasn't hard to imagine the scene that day in 1931 in the New York studio of Walt Kuhn — painter, cyclist and director of *Hitchy-koo*. Ted enviously inhaled the pungent oils, her stage make-up and exposed skin. Kuhn had her perched on an uncomfortable bar stool he'd nabbed from the speakeasy downstairs. Her feathered headdress bobbed and swished as she wriggled on the stool. Ostrich and some sort of parrot. Her gown rustled as she adjusted her pose. She sighed. Flesh jiggled. 'Don't move, honey. Hold it right there. Yep, keep that look. We'll break in a minute.' Walt winked at her. His stubby fingers had paint under the nails. Walt was no chicken, but pretty fit from all that cycling.

THERE was now a scene where Ted, home again, fell into a depression because Lauren hadn't returned his phone calls. He reminded himself that she was in the desert and there would naturally be communication problems and inconvenience. Even so, when he pictured Lauren in the desert on Saturday night she was hardly suffering. He visualised the director, the producer, the agency creative director, the male 'talent', the crew, the Afghan camel drivers, the gorgeous sunset, the party and the high jinks under the clarity of the moon and stars.

He poured himself a drink and flipped through the exhibition catalogue. Yes, there were some major works here. All the nineteenth and twentieth century names: van Gogh, Picasso, Renoir, Monet, Cézanne, Matisse, Manet, Bonnard. The original collector had been a steel magnate from Pittsburgh whose descendents had turned the collection into a public museum. This businessman had responded to their beauty and power whereas he, a creative person, had been more taken by the work of an illustrator! Ted lapsed into self-loathing. He bemoaned his adman's limitations. How he despised his quick acceptance of the facile and vulgar. What a stereotype he was. How apt that his response to the painting of the showgirl had come from his glands. He might as well have spent the afternoon with a copy of *Penthouse*.

On a desperate whim Ted decided to phone Claudia, an old girlfriend. Increasingly, when Lauren was away he thought of Claudia. Claudia's marriage had recently broken up. Various images of her flooded back and he made the call before he could change his mind. He smiled into the phone. He was surprisingly excited but he kept it breezy. 'Hel-*lo*.' he said. 'It's Ted. Have you seen the *Old Masters, New Visions* exhibition?'

'No, not yet.'

'Come with me tomorrow. Everyone's talking about the Bonnards.'

'I'd love to,' she said, 'but I'm seeing a gynaecologist at the moment.'

He gave a startled laugh. 'You're seeing your gynaecologist tomorrow? On a Sunday? Or you're going out with a gynaecologist?'

'Umm, both.'

There was a pause. '*Seeing* him?' His voice was rising. 'You mean professionally *and* sexually?'

'Well, sort of. Yes.'

'The same fellow you used to see? The middle-aged one with the "kind, crinkly eyes"? The one who said you had a lovely uterus?'

She didn't answer.

'I always wondered about him,' he said.

'Yes, well. I've been going to him for years and years. Since way back.'

'Jesus, Claudia, your gynaecologist! Is that ethical?'

'Why not? We're both separated.'

AFTER his abortive conversation with Claudia, Ted called his mother. She was grateful to hear from him, as always, and accepted his invitation to the exhibition with pleasure. Then Ted tried calling the desert again.

The phone rang and rang. He saw it reverberating under the stars, just the phone alone in the gritty wilderness, nothing for a thousand kilometres in any direction but the clamoring telephone. Night animals scuttled from the disturbance. Something sniffed tentatively at it. A dingo, a death adder, a goanna. Some carrion eater pecked at it. Eventually a man answered brusquely, as if he'd been woken suddenly, and said 'the TV people' were 'still out celebrating somewhere.' No, he didn't know where. He had a harsh accent, German or Dutch. 'I'm just trying to run a bloody motel,' he said. 'Fat chance!' He laughed bitterly. 'Never again,' he said, and hung up. Ted threw on a clean shirt and went straight out to Leon's.

Leon's was a nightclub and smart pick-up place. It operated on three levels, with a bistro downstairs, a noisy bar on the next floor and a performing space upstairs. As Ted entered, mawkish, parodic early rock 'n roll songs seeped down from upstairs. Ted climbed the stairs toward the music and bursts of laughter and applause from the audience. On stage were Ward Hopper and the Paper Dolls, a flashily-dressed male singer and his glamorous three-woman backing group. As Ted came into the room they were singing 'Lipstick on Your Collar', dipping and swaying together while maintaining expressions so vacant and soulful that the audience was in stitches.

Ted applauded with the audience as Ward Hopper and the Paper Dolls slid smoothly from one mock-sentimental number to another, from 'It's My Party (And I'll Cry If I Want To)', to 'Save the Last Dance For Me', 'Teen Angel' and 'Tell Laura I Love Her'. But Ted kept his eyes on the Paper Dolls, particularly the

198

middle one. It intrigued him that with each increasingly maudlin number the look of weary pathos on her face become more defined. He was struck by this change in her. Obviously something was on her mind. She wasn't finding the sappy songs ironic any more. Maybe under that deadpan expression she was finding them *sentimental*.

The middle Paper Doll was a dark-haired girl who wore a red strapless dress that showed off her pale rounded shoulders and upper breasts and — assisted by several stiff frilly petticoats that fluffed out like a tutu — her slim legs. Her lips were scarlet. There was a dark central-European cast to her features, a high-cheekboned intensity not quite masked by her stage expression. At the same time her world-weariness was accentuated by the bright make-up and dress and silly song routine. Ted was enraptured by her. At Leon's it was customary for the entertainers to come down to the bar after the show. As soon as the Paper Dolls flounced off stage Ted hurried downstairs. He was sitting at the end of the bar nearest the door, his seat half swivelled towards it, when the middle Paper Doll, more deadpan than ever in street clothes, came in.

The series of snappy scenes that followed — Ted buying her a drink, the pair of them becoming more animated as they hit it off, then leaving the nightclub together, hailing a cab and driving off into the night — made their intention, if not their exact destination, quite clear.

'SHE looks like a drinking woman,' said Ted's mother. They were standing in front of the Bonnards studying

199

Woman with Dog. 'There's even a bottle of wine on the table.'

Ted smiled at his mother and looked carefully at the model, at her flushed face, swollen eyes and vacant expression. 'She looks a bit unhappy,' he said. 'Apparently she was a chronic invalid.'

The stocky guide led a tour group in a flying wedge past Ted and his mother and halted in front of *Woman with Dog*. 'Notice the powerful structure of verticals,' said the guide. 'The woman's nose, the dog's nose and the bottle are lined up in a way that is wittily unorthodox yet formally effective.'

'That's a drinker's face,' his mother said. 'They go into a sort of trance.'

He glanced at the catalogue. 'It was his wife Marthe. You wouldn't pick her for the same woman in *The Open Window* and *The Palm*, would you? And in this nude one. She was an obsessive bather.'

His mother warily regarded the nude woman, legs akimbo, at her toilette. 'He can't have been easy to live with,' she said. 'The painter.'

'It says here that he adored her,' Ted said. '"Her self-absorption, which drove away Bonnard's friends, made her an ideal subject for him to study. He was a painter of moods and she created them."'

His mother was looking past him toward the Renoirs. 'Now, they're pretty,' she said. Reluctantly she turned back to the Bonnards. 'Imagine being spied on all day long. No wonder she drank.'

'He loved her,' Ted said. 'For fifty years.' She was edging past him to the Renoirs. 'I thought you'd like these,' he said, a little peevishly. 'The love story behind them.'

200

'No, these are my pick,' she said. 'I love these. It's just like you're having lunch with them, isn't it?'

'Yes,' he said. He gave a little anticipatory shiver. He was keeping the best till last. It was like being at a crowded party with the knowledge that your new and secret lover was across the room. It was just a matter of time. It was delicious to stretch it out like this. They paused in front of the van Goghs, the Matisses, the Modiglianis, the Monets and Manets, the Cézannes and Picassos. Slowly, almost luxuriously, he turned towards the Americans.

'I hate that one,' his mother said.

'*Showgirl with Plumes*,' he said, not batting an eye.

OUTSIDE the gallery they sauntered along through the park while he kept an eye out for a taxi. They were scarce on a Sunday afternoon but there was no particular hurry. 'Tell me one thing,' his mother said, hooking her arm through his. 'When am I going to meet your friend? Lauren.'

'Oh, that's more or less over,' he said. When she said nothing he went on, 'You know actresses.'

A cab cruised past then and he hailed it. He reached out and opened the back door for her. When they were settled inside she tapped his nearest hand with a schoolmarmish finger. 'You need someone to keep you up to scratch,' she said. 'What's that brown stuff under your nails?'

'Paint,' he said. Nonchalantly he hid his fingernails by making his hands into fists. He lay them loosely on his knees. 'Just paint.'

Arrows

JUST when Ed is thinking that Vincent's heart isn't in the Hong Kong nightclub milieu to which he seems so suited, Vincent starts socialising with nightclub performers in his own home! In daylight! For now there are shots of showgirl-looking women taken against the backdrop of a sparsely furnished living room — not this comfortably appointed apartment in Stanley Beach Road but a typical young buck's bachelor flat.

But the cast and their actions are atypical. These are mature women. There is a black woman bearing her breasts. Standing alone and smiling, she has the look of an off-duty stripper — but one with weighty matters on her mind. There is another shot of the same woman in naked profile, her face serious and striving for an 'arty' look — her breast silhouetted on the wall behind her — which is spoiled by the edge of a TV set and half a venetian blind poking into the photograph.

Against the same backdrop, a bare-breasted white woman, a redhead, is now kissing Vincent. Although she is almost naked she, too, gives the impression of being in 'civvies'. She is taller than Vincent, with pale breasts and a sprinkling of orange freckles on her shoulders and upper arms. Her hands tenderly hold his head while she kisses him on the mouth. But the effect is more maternal than erotic because *his* hands hang by his sides.

Next, Vincent is sprawled on a chair dressed only in a pair of black briefs. He looks stoned. His body is as thin as a fourteen-year-old's. On the floor in front of him, strangely pathetic, lie his boots, burgundy-colored and, with their high heels, very dated-looking.

(This is the only picture in which Vincent seems to have dropped his guard. But the fact that he has included it in his album indicates that he is quite happy with the effect it presents.)

And now the scene shifts outdoors. It looks like the morning or, more likely, the afternoon after the events in the flat. The cast is the same.

Again it is the redhead making the more intimate contact with Vincent. Wearing a diaphanous peasant blouse and with her sunglasses pushed back on her hair, she is kissing him in the middle of the street. The street climbs up a hill. Both man and woman are very aware of the camera. Vincent is fondling her bare midriff in a gesture perhaps intended to shock or impress the Chinese passersby, four men and a small boy, who have stopped to goggle at their display. (An old Chinese woman hurries past, looking straight ahead.) The redhead is standing with her legs spread wide to bring her down to Vincent's height. Vincent looks sharp and casual out-of-doors. He's dressed completely in denim and his shirt is unbuttoned almost to the waist. The hand on her midriff, his stance, are cocky and possessive. Today he is in control of events.

Between photographs the camera must have been passed from the black woman to the redhead because now Vincent stands with an arm looped around the black woman's hip. A minute or two have passed. The Chinese males still gawp at them, but from a vantage point twenty or thirty metres further up the hill.

*   *   *

NEXT morning, a Saturday, Fiona came for the rent and Vincent's mail. She was a tall fair girl, broad-shouldered, tanned, with a smart London accent and a white Saab. She spoke for some time to Sally in the kitchen, then strolled into the living room, calling over her shoulder, 'Do you mind if I take the exercise bench? I'm just piling on the pudding around the middle.'

The exercise bench stood among a stack of gym equipment in a corner of the terrace, a jumble of steel and chrome and padded vinyl. Ed extracted it and helped her down the stairs with it into the heat. He noticed that her stomach was actually trim and flat. Fiona jammed the American Express bills into a pocket of her shorts. 'Just passing through, are you?' she said.

When he came back upstairs, Andrea said, 'She's a shrewd one.' Andrea was drinking fruit juice on the terrace with her legs up, and flicking through *Kaiser's Speak-Easy Cantonese*.

Ed was sweating and puffing slightly. He sat beside her. 'What do you think Vincent's in for? Drugs? Some sort of corruption?'

'A white-collar crime. I don't know, fraud?' Under the heading *General*, Kaiser listed the words 'prophylactic' and 'public holiday' together. Andrea read them out: *'bay yahn doy'* and *'gah kay'*, bravely attempting the sing-song voice tones.

'He's a driven man,' Ed said. 'I know it. He's living some sort of lie.'

The sounds making up the Cantonese word for prophylactic were broken up into three voice tones. *'Bay'* had a normal tone but *'yahn'* was supposed to have a low voice tone and *'doy'* a high rising tone. The changes in voice tone were represented by Kaiser as arrows. There were arrows for high ↑, low ↓, falling \\, low rising ⟋ and high rising ⟋ tones. Tiny arrows — not only for the voice tones for prophylactic and public holiday but for the sounds of every conceivable requirement and negotiation — plunged and soared all over the booklet.

'You're funny,' Andrea said. 'You fellows.'

'It's interesting. The whole situation's interesting,' Ed said.

'Dear heart, why don't you take it easy?' From the terrace Andrea watched the crowds swimming and paddling down at Stanley Beach. A lifeguard moved slowly among the swimmers, rowing a strange umbrella-covered craft with two hulls. From here the raft didn't seem so far out in the bay, she thought, maybe two hundred metres. Although the water there was more than deep enough, the lifeguard's main task seemed to be to prevent young men diving from the raft. He would row slowly out to it and shoo them off, then row sedately back to shore under his umbrella, by which time the men would be diving off the raft once more. So the lifeguard would row out to the raft again. Everyone looked content with the arrangement.

In the mood she was in it seemed to Andrea a leisurely and satisfactory way of keeping the lifeguard employed and exercised and the men entertained. She went to get her camera.

SALLY had taken the job in Hong Kong to escape finally from the White Prince, a married actor whose heroic mien and many Shakespearean roles had given him a public probity at odds with his four-year inability to, as she told him, 'either shit or get off the pot'.

By Sunday morning, however, Australia, *home*, was bearing the brunt of her firm and, in her friends' view, debatable, decision. The White Prince's prevarication, the Green Dwarf's ignorance, even, perhaps, the Black Knave's insouciance, had been somehow transferred on to the country itself.

'So what's been going on at home?' she asked. For an hour she'd been edgy, pacing the terrace with a cigarette and a fierce smile. 'Rapes galore, from what I read.' She fluffed out her hair from her neck. 'Fill me in.'

'Where do I start?' Andrea said. 'The murder of the nurse? The young schoolteacher on the train?'

Sally broke in. 'Well, how far would *you* go? Would you lie back and enjoy it? Put up a bit of a scuffle and then give in? What?'

Andrea glanced across at Ed and widened her eyes. 'I wouldn't give in without a fight,' she said.

'So he kills you,' Sally said. 'Terrific.'

'What if you gave in meekly without a fight and he killed you anyway?' Andrea said.

'What would it matter then?'

Andrea looked out across the bay. 'I'd rather go out as good as possible.'

'Hmm,' said Sally. 'We don't get too many maniacs here, you know. That's something I'll say for Hong Kong.' Then she looked over to Andrea and smiled. 'I love the way you're worried about going out *good. Good.* What a virtuous little actress you are, darling.'

'Sal!'

Sally stepped briskly inside, then came out with the

drinks tray. 'I'm way out of touch,' she said. 'I'd love to hear your definition of *good* one day when you've got time.'

It took lunch at the Cricket Club to lighten Sally's mood. While they were picking at their cold collations she giggled and produced an air-mail edition of *The Times* pilfered from the reading room. 'I have an announcement to make,' she said in dulcet tones. 'The Princess Anne, Mrs Mark Phillips, this afternoon opened and toured the new unit of L & K Fertilisers Limited at Sharpness, Gloucestershire.' She glanced imperiously around the dining room. 'Mrs Timothy Holderness Roddam was in attendance.'

'I love it!' she said. She made her accent primmer. Some of the diners began to turn towards her. She went on. 'By command of the Queen, Lieutenant-Colonel the Lord Charteris of Amisfield, permanent Lord in Waiting, was present at Heathrow Airport this afternoon upon the departure of the Duke of Kent, accompanied by the Earl of St Andrews, for Botswana. Botswana!' Sally was still hooting when a committee-man came over, frowning, and spoke to her.

When he left she sipped her wine and giggled self-consciously. 'I should tell you something. I've given up feminism.'

'You what?' Andrea said.

'It's no way to get a man.' Sally giggled again. Her meal was still untouched. 'Why stab yourself in the back?'

'Sally!' said Andrea.

Ed held up his hands. 'I'm saying nothing,' he said.

Sally said, 'There's this mountain on the mainland, in China, that spinsters climb. They come from all over the country to burn incense and pray for a husband. I went over last weekend with a couple of friends in a similar position. Theatrical *personnel* like myself. We took a picnic and made a day of it. We were joking around to start with, but we climbed the mountain, we burned the incense. We got deadly serious.'

'Time to come home, Sally,' Andrea said.

'I'm nice to them all now, shits and all.'

'I can't believe what I'm hearing,' Andrea said.

'One factor that I didn't consider when I came here,' Sally said, 'was that the local men would not appeal.'

'Ah,' said Ed.

'So then you're stuck with the expatriates, all very dull and pukka. Do you know?' she said, waving her wine glass, 'that as I get older the men that interest me most are the laboring types.' Her voice had risen again and people were turning around and muttering. A woman said something sharp in an English accent. 'Businessmen are *just* acceptable,' Sally said. 'But definitely no intellectuals. No one sensitive or arty. No-one studenty or punkish. No one in black clothes. I don't want to bloody *talk* any more.'

'No actors?' Ed said.

'Cross actors right off the list.' She gulped some wine. 'Actors don't get *on* the fucking list.'

Maybe the surrounding English accents were contagious. Andrea's voice sounded as if she were on stage. 'So you want *precisely* the type you'd avoid back home?' she said.

'Not any more, I wouldn't,' Sally said.

ON the drive home from the Cricket Club Andrea was subdued and Ed shifted restlessly on the back seat as

Sally negotiated the dips and bends of Stanley Beach Road with an expression of strained amusement on her face. But as they came into the apartment they were jolted into panic by a swarm of hornets in the kitchen. In the hubbub, before the gardener got them outside and closed the windows on them, a stray hornet stung Sally on the forehead. As Andrea fetched some ice cubes for the sting she called out, 'Divine retribution, I'd call it.'

'I'm speechless,' Sally said. 'I cannot and will not speak.'

As dusk fell Ed stood on the terrace watching the junks light their lanterns. The view of the bay, the tropical smells, the blood temperature of the air, had become familiar in two days. He went inside, poured a glass of wine and took down the album from the bookcase. He still felt restless and disappointed at the day's lack of exotica. In a new place he didn't like to waste a day. While he flipped through the album the women came into the room and collapsed on the settee. They leaned back, sighing and fanning air up their legs.

Sally's left eye was almost closed from the sting. Her other eye spotted the gecko on the ceiling. 'Where were you during the hornet invasion?' she said.

'Do they eat hornets?' Andrea said.

'Why not?' Sally said.

'I think the swelling has stopped now,' Andrea said.

'You're kidding!'

'Stopped getting any bigger, I mean.'

Ed glanced up from the album for a second. 'It's definitely going down,' he said. A spark of excitement lit up his face. Just as he was nearing the end of the album there was Vincent suddenly presenting a different image altogether. Vincent was shifting ground, moving on.

Vincent sat behind a typewriter. He was taking an active role. In the background were filing cabinets and three newsroom clocks showing different times, labelled *New York*, *London* and *Hong Kong*. Suddenly Vincent was more mature and more conservatively dressed. He looked to be in his early thirties, amiable but determined. He looked more masculine and more solidly built. (The gym equipment on the terrace?) The sleeves of his business shirt were rolled up, two or three crisp turns. His collar and tie were loosened. He looked like an ace reporter. What a good sport to halt his scoop-writing for a quick snap!

But his cigarillo was wrong. There was also no paper in the typewriter.

Ed noticed another modification to Vincent's image. His taste in women had changed. There were no more strippers and showgirls. No-one with the nightclub look. He had turned to middle-class English-looking girls, fresh-faced Cricket Club types, the adventurous daughters of dentists and stockbrokers working their way around the Commonwealth. And among these Anglo-Saxon stenographers laughing with Vincent on the Star ferry, sipping drinks in Macau, was an easily recognisable Fiona in a green bikini beside a swimming pool, her firm stomach tanned and shiny with oil.

'This bastard is up to something,' Ed said. He was elated. What could he have him do now? How would the script proceed? He thought: he has to get out of jail; his presence has to touch the lovers' lives. 'What do you think, Sally?'

She paid no attention. Andrea had begun rubbing lotion into her swollen forehead. Sally immediately started making little girlish intakes of breath. She winced and gasped like a five-year-old. Andrea soothed her with even softer strokes. She clucked and shooshed. 'Sore, sore,' Sally murmured, and her head, like a cat's, followed eagerly after Andrea's strokes, loth for them to end.

There were no more photographs in the album. Ed put it on the floor and drank some wine. The attention being paid to Sally's sting made conversation difficult. He began to feel uneasy and superfluous. This was becoming a difficult film to plot.

He tried to consider the scene as it was unfolding: a detailed and complex — though wordless — conversation was taking place in the living room of an apartment in Hong Kong while a man, frowning, quickly drank the remainder of his wine and one woman administered to another. This silent discussion was conducted — with questioning glances from the man, and deliberately mannered and sometimes obtuse responses from the women — to the accompaniment of a female country singer crooning of soured love.

To an onlooker the man's side of the 'conversation' would have been the easiest to follow. His confused looks and speedy gestures asked, What are you doing? And why are you ignoring me? Okay, he would pretend he wasn't seeing what he was seeing.

Her swollen eye gave one of the women great kudos. To the man it seemed to say, We know things you don't. But the other woman's impassive face said plainly, Why are you acting so strangely here?

The man's increasingly bewildered and petulant

211

expression, on the other hand, seemed to ask, Why are you two in cahoots against me? And why are you stroking her? She's old enough to rub on her own antihistamine ointment.

Then the swollen eye became very smug. The other woman's frown said, Why don't you go to bed? Instead, the man poured another glass of wine and stretched back defiantly in his chair as if he were waiting them out. The lovelorn singer whined on. The only question still in the man's eyes was wary and oblique and impossible to ever voice.

Wordless conversations, too, come to a natural conclusion. Andrea's strokes became slower, shorter, until with a final pat she finished caressing Sally's forehead. Sally sat up briskly and poured herself another wine. She turned to Ed. Her left eye was villainous, a piratical slit, but her good eye was shining. Smiling broadly, she raised her glass in a toast. 'To absent friends.'

'Absent friends,' Andrea replied.

Ed glanced at Andrea for a moment and then turned towards the bay. 'Yeah,' he said.

Sally was still looking at him and smiling. 'Ed, I have another photo. A more recent one.'

'I'm not really interested,' he said.

'The best one yet,' Sally said.

'Show me,' Andrea said, and reached across for the photograph.

Ed was still intently watching Andrea's expression when suddenly, in the sing-song voice tone, she sang out, 'Bay yahn doy!' Again, 'Bay yahn doy!' On the 'doy' her voice, controlled and professional, rose high in her head. Rampant arrows zipped through the humid air and shot around the room.